W9-BNS-446

Handbook for Dragon Slayers

ALSO BY MERRIE HASKELL

The Princess Curse

Handbook for Dragon Slayers

MERRIE HASKELL

HARPER
An Imprint of HarperCollins*Publishers*

Handbook for Dragon Slayers
 For information address HarperCollins Children's Books, a division of HarperCollins Publishers, 10 East 53rd Street, New York, NY 10022.
www.harpercollins.com

Library of Congress Cataloging-in-Publication Data
Haskell, Merrie.
Handbook for dragon slayers / Merrie Haskell. — 1st ed.
p. cm.
Summary: Yearning for life in a cloistered scriptorium, thirteen-year-old Princess Matilda, whose lame foot brings fear of the evil eye, escapes her scheming cousin Ivo and joins her servant Judith and an old friend, Parz, in hunting dragons and writing about them.
ISBN 978-0-06-200816-9 (hardcover bdg.)
[1. Fairy tales. 2. Adventure and adventurers—Fiction. 3. Princesses—Fiction. 4. People with disabilities—Fiction. 5. Dragons—Fiction. 6. Authorship—Fiction. 7. Books and reading—Fiction.]
I. Title.
PZ8.H2563Han 2013 2012022159
[Fic]—dc23 CIP
AC

Typography by Carla Weise
14 15 16 17 LP/RRDH 10 9 8 7 6 5 4 3 2

First Edition

For my mother,

Beverly Cook,

who taught me the keywords for this book:

RESILIENCE *and* TRANSFORMATION *and* LOVE

(and many other words besides,

as well as how to spell them)

WHOSOEVER STEALS THIS BOOK
shall BURN *in the*
Fiery Conflagration *of a*
Dragon's Breath
and will also
Lose Their Nose
to
Putrefaction.
It is advised, therefore,
that you take your
nose home intact,
and leave this HANDBOOK
for the study of proper
Dragon Slayers.

chapter 1

"THAT'S THE SIXTH KNOCK THIS MORNING. I WISH I lived in a cave!"

"Because caves don't have doors?" asked Judith, my handmaiden, rising to answer the knock.

I nearly threw down my pen in disgust, but that would have splattered my parchment and ruined hours of work. It also wouldn't be behavior suitable for a princess.

"Yes," I said, and settled for tucking my pen behind my ear in the exact way that infuriated my mother because it left large ink blotches on my neck. "I'm never going to finish this copy in time."

"Ahem," Judith said. "You do realize that even with your mother gone for a week, I'm still going to scrub you pink and inkless on bath day."

I rubbed the numb spot where my braids pulled my scalp, hoping my inky fingers left a blotch there, too. "I do realize it."

"Well, take pity on your ink scrubber, then," she said, and opened the door to reveal Horrible Hermannus, landed knight, estate steward of Alder Brook, and my life's bane. He was wearing a tunic of goose-turd green, a color that no cloth should ever be dyed.

Horrible Hermannus nodded to Judith and bowed to me. "Princess Matilda, I've a message from Sir Kunibert of Boar House. He begs Alder Brook's assistance with the coming tax."

I wiped my fingers on my blotting rag, trying to hide my sudden despair.

"Sir Kunibert needs help?" I asked with forced calm. "How much help?" Alder Brook had no coin to spare for Sir Kunibert's coffers, no matter how desperate he might be.

"He needs assistance with his record keeping, as I am sure there hasn't been any in years," Horrible said. "He would need two days' worth of aid, perhaps? But of course that is impossible with your mother gone. I will relay to Sir Kunibert that we cannot consider his request until Princess Isobel returns on Friday."

My despair seeped away like rain soaking into dry

earth, to be replaced by growing excitement. "No," I said, sitting straighter on my stool. "I'll go. I'll help Sir Kunibert."

Two days at Boar House! Boar House meant Parz—I hadn't seen Parz in *weeks*. I tried to hide the eagerness I now felt by putting on a studied frown.

"I'll start packing," Judith said immediately, and bustled off to pull out a traveling chest.

"Princess, wait," Horrible said. "Even if Alder Brook could spare you—what about the emperor's gift? I would be remiss not to point out that you have less than nine weeks till New Year's."

My excitement was checked, and my gaze fell on the half-finished page on my desk. I was copying *On Horsemanship* as Alder Brook's New Year gift to the emperor. While I loved copying books, even ones about horses, the constant interruptions had turned this pleasure into a burden.

"Rationally speaking, if I copy early in the mornings at Boar House, without the interruptions I experience here, I might well *gain* pages, not lose them, by being away."

I spoke calmly and thoughtfully, even as my mind raced ahead, coming up with argument and counterargument. We *had* to go to Boar House. It was the only chance to see Parz until maybe Christmas.

Horrible glanced down at my sloped writing desk,

clearly weighing issues in the balance. "Sir Kunibert may not owe allegiance to Alder Brook, but he is our neighbor," he said. "And he is the closest dragon slayer by far; Alder Brook would suffer if the emperor imprisoned him. But Princess, if you think someone should go to Boar House before your mother returns, let it be me or the chamberlain. I don't know if your mother—"

"My mother isn't here," I said—not sharply, but serenely, as befits a princess.

Horrible's lip twitched in annoyance, but he bowed his acquiescence. I tried to hide a smile. "There's been a new dragon sighted at Mount Lorelei," he said. "And we can't afford to lose even two cows to a dragon. One, maybe. But not two. I'm sure Princess Isobel will see the urgency."

"Yes, of course," I said, satisfied but deflated all at once. "We can't lose any cows." I sighed. Why did being a princess always come down to taxes and cows?

"I'll see to your boat," Horrible said, dashing off another stupid little bow and going out. I scowled at his retreating back.

"Don't make that face, Tilda," Judith said, tucking freshly laundered chemises into the chest. "He was very nice to you just now. Your mother is going to question him thoroughly about why he let you go."

True. My mother didn't like me to travel, saying it was too dangerous, and bad for my foot besides; in fact, I had only ever journeyed a day up and down the Victory River by boat.

"Horrible's not going to wait for her questions," I said, corking my inkhorn. "He's going to tattle as soon as Mother returns. He has all the sense of fair play of a three-year-old child."

"*Sir Hermannus* is obligated to keep you safe," Judith said, lifting a sleeping cat off my fur robe and cuddling the cat briefly. "And he's obligated to obey your mother in all things."

Also true, but it didn't make me like Horrible any better. He had an uncanny knack for getting me in trouble with my mother. When I was younger, I thought he kept a hearthgoblin to spy on me.

I slid from my stool, testing my leg and foot after the morning's inactivity. My leg trembled briefly, wanting to cramp, but it held. The pain on the walking surface of my foot was tolerable today; I had been sitting a lot, with all the copy work, and my latest sore had healed.

I left my crutch at the desk and hitch-stepped over to Judith, lifting my arms so she could help me remove my ink-splotched, donkey-gray gown.

Judith bent her head over the side ties on my gown, but even at that awkward angle, I caught the expression on her face. "You're smirking," I accused.

"Only because *you* were blushing from the

moment Sir Hermannus mentioned Boar House."

Oh. "I wasn't," I mumbled. But Judith had been my handmaiden since she was nine and I was seven; even with six years of practice, I sometimes failed at hiding my stronger emotions from her.

"Your cheeks are still rosy." She pulled the gown over my head. "I guessed right—you want to see Lord Parzifal!"

I took a deep breath to steady my voice. "Lord Parzifal will doubtless be busy with his training."

"Even Sir Kunibert doesn't train his squires in the dark." Judith laced me into a pretty robe of celestrine-blue silk. "And Lord Parzifal will have to come in for supper. And that might very well lead to a *conversation*." She grinned at me.

I wrinkled my nose at her. "I have to pack my writing box now."

"I'm not stopping you," she said, and busied herself with our toiletries.

I turned back to my writing corner. The private rooms of a prince's keep performed double, if not triple, duty. This room was my mother's bower and ran half the length of the great hall below it. Here I slept with my mother and our principal servants; I wrote letters and copied manuscripts at the window; and my mother's ladies sewed all day by the fire, from tapestry work to the plainest mending. The bower was large, as befitted a principality of Alder Brook's stature—and yet it felt terribly crowded most of the time.

With Mother gone for a week, I luxuriated in sprawling bed space, with Judith my only roommate. It felt shameful to waste any of our last few days alone by going to Boar House, where we'd have to sleep cheek by jowl with the female servants.

But I had enjoyed my mother's absence for more than just bed space in the bower. Until I married or turned twenty-one, I had to defer to my mother as my regent. This week was the first time I had been free of her constant instruction since . . .

Since before my father left on pilgrimage to take back the Holy Land.

For the first time in two years, I hadn't had to endure a morning lecture on my duty. *Everything*, as it happened, was my duty, from balancing accounts to writing flattering letters to emperors and archbishops to wearing my hair in two neat plaits. Basically, my duty consisted of just about everything I didn't want to do and nothing I did want to do.

Since I *wanted* to go to Boar House, it couldn't possibly be the right thing to do. But I was going anyway.

I tidied up my little work corner, shuffling parchments into piles, putting away extra pens, knives, inks, and sands that I wouldn't take to Sir Kunibert's. I closed up the book I had been copying from, worried how it might fare on the boat.

Anxiously, I triple-wrapped the book: first in linen, then in two layers of oilcloth. Alder Brook could never afford to replace *On Horsemanship* without an exceptionally good harvest—which this year had not granted us. I had a momentary twinge of guilt at the thought of endangering the book. But—Horrible hadn't told me no.

Once the original book was wrapped, I looked over my page of copying. I wondered if I really was going to be able to finish the copy by New Year's with the small time I was allowed to devote to it and all the interruptions I'd encountered. It had been my suggestion to send a book to the emperor. I still wasn't sure why my mother had agreed, other than that the gift would look much more expensive than anything else Alder Brook could give.

My other reasons for wanting to make the copy were selfish, however. I wanted a chance to work with all that pristine parchment, of course, and the chance to lay out a book. And I also wanted the leftover materials that such a large undertaking would surely supply.

Something horrifying caught my eye:

A damp and smooth floor may be the ruin of a naturally good hoof. A damp and smooth floor may be the ruin of a naturally good hoof.

I gasped. I'd written the same sentence *twice*. And there was no going back and scraping just that sentence out—it was right in the middle of the page. And scraping a whole page after the ink had dried—there was no hope for it. You could always see the ghost of the words you'd written underneath the new lettering, and that would never do in a gift for the emperor. I groaned and put a hand over my eyes.

"What's wrong, Tilda?" Judith asked.

"I ruined a page," I said tightly. "The whole leaf, really, because if we cut out the bad page, it will look *so* obvious when the book is bound. It wouldn't have happened if I weren't interrupted all the time." I wanted to ball the parchment up and throw it, but that would be beyond wasteful. Even if this leaf couldn't go into the book, we would use the parchment to write a letter or something, after we scraped it.

But saving the parchment didn't save the work. Hours of effort—wasted. Gone.

I swallowed my anger and disappointment and scraped quickly at the words, destroying my morning's work. What I couldn't remove now would have to be pumiced off later.

"Tilda, aren't we going?" Judith asked. She pointed to the clothes chest. She had left just enough room for my writing box.

"I can't leave this for two days," I said. "The longer the ink sits, the deeper it sinks into the parchment. You go on ahead—take the book and the clothes chest down to the boat. I'll bring my writing box in just a moment."

She nodded, closed the chest, and hoisted it to her shoulder, then tucked the book under an arm. Another half bow, and she was gone.

I scraped carefully with my curved knife, silently seething . . . and couldn't help but think that life would be so much easier if I lived in a cloister. I could copy every day in a silent, spacious scriptorium. Even if I ruined a page, a day like today wouldn't seem so bad if there were a hundred tomorrows of peace and quiet.

Eventually, the page was as bare as I could make it. I packed up the rest of my writing box and headed out.

I had just cracked the door when I heard Father Ripertus's voice on the stairs. I'd been unable to run around as a little child, so Father Ripertus had taught me reading and the methods of scribes so that I might not sit idle. He was my confessor, and one of my favorite people.

"—the Illustrious Isobel's true mission has failed,"

Father Ripertus said. He was talking to Horrible and scanning a letter in his hand. "The lord of Larkspur will not betroth his son to Princess Mathilda."

I froze, the door but inches open. A betrothal! Thank heaven nothing had come of it—my cousin Ivo was an idiot I had no use for—but why had my mother told me the purpose of her trip was to check on the grape harvests upriver?

"The foot, of course," Horrible said in a sour voice.

Father Ripertus coughed slightly.

"Not the foot?" Horrible sounded surprised.

"Not *just* the foot. Those rumors don't help anything," Father Ripertus said.

"Ah, yes," Horrible said, and I thought I could not have hated him more than at that moment. He spoke so resignedly, as though he knew all about all the rumors, whatever they were—I could only assume they were about Alder Brook's bare treasury. I shifted my weight uncomfortably off my foot and tried to hope people weren't saying stupid things about *it* instead. "Princess Isobel is coming home early, then?" Horrible asked.

Father Ripertus's shoulders hunched. "No—here's what I really came to tell you: She has broken her leg! The bonesetter will not let her stir from Larkspur until after Christmas."

I veered dizzily between urgent worry and sudden

glee that my mother would *finally* understand what it was like to be unable to trust her feet. Like me.

Worry won out, though, and easily. It had been too few months since the day we received word from the Holy Land about my father's death in battle; the thought of my mother lying injured and alone reopened the cold, empty spot that had hollowed me out that day.

I sucked in my cheeks and smoothed the wrinkles of concern off my face before opening the door wider. The first rule of princessing is to be in control of oneself at all times. A princess never shows unnecessary emotion.

Horrible and Father Ripertus jerked around to face me as I came through the door.

"Is my mother all right?" I asked, and cursed inwardly when my voice proved less reliable than my face. "It must be pretty bad if she doesn't insist on a litter to bring her home. . . ."

"Tilda, Tilda," Father Ripertus soothed, folding his letter and slipping it into his sleeve. "Your mother is choosing for the first time to take the advice of a physician for herself. That is more a cause for celebration than alarm."

It *was* unlike her to do what a physician recommended, no matter how much pain she was in. The only reason she might do that was if it served another purpose. "She has been saying she needs to spend more time overseeing the eastern holdings," I said slowly. "Maybe this is partly an excuse." I didn't mention overhearing their discussion of my betrothal. Or nonbetrothal, as it stood.

"Ah. There. You have guessed her motivations, I'm sure quite accurately," Father Ripertus said.

Horrible hesitated, mouth half open as if he wanted to say something, but then he bowed, backing down the stairs. "Forgive me, Princess. I only came to say your boat is ready." He swiftly departed.

I was left alone at the top of the stairs with Father Ripertus, who had managed to summon up a reassuring and kindly expression.

"She *will* be fine, Tilda," Father Ripertus said, putting a warm hand on my head. "She's still on Alder Brook lands—she'll come to no real harm." I wanted to lean into his hand and accept his comfort; I also wanted to believe him. It was a nice fairy story, to think that our borders marked the line between safety and danger.

I forced a smile. "Of course she'll be fine. Thank you." We nodded to each other, and he went back down the stairs, a dissatisfied cast to his lips.

I leaned against the bower door, clutching my writing box, and closed my eyes. I imagined myself in a clean cloister scriptorium. Life would be so much easier there. To spend every day alone with acres of parchment and rivers of ink—in a place like that, bad news would seem far away, like it didn't matter.

I drew in a deep breath, opening my eyes. My mother was going to be all right. Everything was going to be fine. Nothing would be made better by either staying here or rushing off to Larkspur. Nothing would be solved by leaving Sir Kunibert's accounts in turmoil.

"All right, then," I breathed, and went downstairs.

I had to descend slowly, one step at a time like a child, to avoid pain or, worse, falling. Stairs always made me feel ungainly, and I hated them.

In the great hall, a wave of silence spread before me as my presence brought all conversation to a halt. Alder Brook's various retainers and servants looked up from their whetstones, from their preparations for the day's dinner, from all the little tasks that had brought them to the great hall, and watched in silence as I toiled across the room.

One servant, a girl named Roswitha, made the sign against the evil eye as I passed.

I made my face smooth like ice, and pretended not to see.

chapter 2

I am sure Roswitha truly thought I did not see her; she made the sign, flicking her fingers over and over, until Frau Aleidis grabbed her hands. Someone in the hall stifled a cough, or maybe a snort.

A hot-cold flash of emotions swept over me—embarrassment, shame, rage. I summoned the memory of my mother's voice in my ear, reminding me that Alder Brook was my freehold and my responsibility, that Alder Brook's people were my people, even if they thought my lame foot brought down the evil eye.

But the memory of my mother's voice wasn't enough. It wasn't nearly enough to allow me to ignore Roswitha. The mask of ice I imagined on my face only saved the world from me; to save me from the world, I had to imagine iron bands around my chest to protect my heart.

Once outside the keep, the pressure on my heart did not ease. In the distance, a group of small children played a variety of tag—only one boy had a tree branch shoved in his armpit, and he was pretending to limp as he chased the other shrieking children. He was pretending to be me.

I couldn't get to the boat landing fast enough. When I climbed into Aged Arnolt's boat, my lame leg shivered and gave out. I crumpled gracelessly into the bow.

Judith made a concerned cluck from behind me, but there was nothing for her to do, and I couldn't talk yet without crying. So I ignored her.

Aged Arnolt turned blank, impassive eyes to the far shore and rowed us across the Victory River. Judith and I didn't speak. We had learned at an early age how easily sound carries across water; we knew that even a quiet conversation would float right to listening ears.

All I could do was stare at the receding walls of my home. Alder Brook Keep was a *wasserschloss*, a water castle, and its outer stone walls came right down to the river's edge, where a rippled mirror image was reflected.

Everyone always said it was a pretty castle. I'd

never thought so; the gray stone walls were square and heavy. I thought the keep looked like a prison, and I wished I didn't have to return to it.

Aged Arnolt let the current do most of the work in crossing to Sir Kunibert's manor. Soon enough, the boat nosed the shallows, and Judith hopped out to grab the prow and haul it in before reaching to help me. Arnolt handed up my crutch without a word.

"Thank you for the smooth journey, Arnolt," I said, because princesses should show gratitude.

Arnolt nodded briefly, not meeting my gaze.

He wouldn't even speak to me. I jammed my crutch under my arm and stalked away from the river. I did not look back, just in case Arnolt was also making the sign against the evil eye.

"Tilda," Judith said, hand on my arm, "you were so excited to come to Boar House. What happened? What's wrong?"

I wanted to tell Judith everything: overhearing Father Ripertus and the refused betrothal and "the rumors"—whatever they were exactly—and also about the sign against the evil eye and the limping boy. But what good would telling her do? It would all just make her angry, too.

So I told her the important part, about my mother's broken leg, and how she was going to spend a long time at Larkspur, recuperating.

"Say the word and we'll go to her," Judith said. "You know how good we are at nursing creatures back to health! Think of all the babies we've rescued."

She meant baby squirrels and fledgling birds and kittens and—most memorably for the punishment we'd received for trying to keep them under the bed—goat kids.

"No—no. That's . . ." I couldn't even think of the word. Impractical? Impossible? Dangerous? It would certainly get us into more trouble than just running off to help out Boar House for a few days. "That's not a good idea." How would we even get there? Larkspur didn't lie on the river. I'd have to take a litter, since riding a horse with my foot was out of the question.

"You're sure?" Judith asked.

I nodded. "There's nothing we can do for her that Larkspur's physician won't do; and yelling at us wouldn't be good for her, anyway." We stood outside the door of Boar House, which was open to let the bright autumn sunshine in.

Judith gave me a reassuring smile, and together we crossed the threshold.

Sir Kunibert, a knight of five-and-fifty, was a free-holder. He held his house-fief by right of property, same as my family; but he had no vassals to speak of and claimed only the lands he could see out his window.

This was a sharp contrast to Alder Brook. Alder Brook Keep was four times the size of Boar House, and the farmlands we held directly amounted to two thousand acres. The whole of the principality of Alder Brook measured maybe twelve leagues across: You could ride a fast horse from one edge of Alder Brook's holdings to the other inside a day, but it had to be a sturdy animal, and you wouldn't take it back the other direction without a day's rest.

Inside, Boar House had one feature that made it impressive in a way that Alder Brook Keep never would be. Sir Kunibert should have renamed the place Dragon House, for the dried head of every single one of his slain dragons hung in his hall.

Sir Kunibert tromped in from the practice field, mud up to his knees, shortly after our arrival. He interviewed me with short, sharp sentences: Did I need parchment? Did I need pens? Did I really need to *talk* to him, or could I read through all his contracts and receipts and just figure it all out? I was given a chest full of jumbled papers and codices, and he went back out to the practice field.

And with that, I was left to it.

I found it creepy to work with half a dozen dragon heads staring down from their sunken eyepits. I faced the opposite wall, which was lined instead with deer antlers and boar tusks—hundreds of them. Or maybe thousands of them, for they not only lined the walls but crept onto the ceiling as well.

At least the antlers and the tusks didn't have empty eye sockets, like the dragon heads.

Judith brought me a pair of fresh tallow candles, then went to ensure our sleeping quarters would be relatively vermin-free. She had stowed some fumigants in our luggage—big bundles of sage, santolina, bay laurel, and rosemary, whose fragrant smoke should drive off most bugs. "Don't forget to stretch your leg," she reminded me as she left.

I frowned, biting back a sharp retort. I had long ago learned not to take out my frustrations on Judith. Yelling at Judith was the only thing my mother had ever punished me for directly, instead of just sending me off to confess to Father Ripertus, but in truth, it was the only thing my mother didn't *need* to punish me for. I had felt so awful, the first and only time I'd yelled at Judith, that I had tried to give her the circlet off my head in apology.

She had wisely refused the circlet, and Judith's mother, Frau Aleidis, had intervened to keep me from pushing it on her.

Instead of snapping, I forced myself to smile and said, "I'll take a break every other contract." I reached into the chest, fighting to untwine the ribbons and ribbons of dangling seals from each other.

"All right. Your crutch is against the wall, behind you."

After she left, I finally got a contract free. It was an agreement about a benefice that included an apple orchard and ten tenant farmers—I was wrong, then, and Boar House did have more land than Sir Kunibert could see from his windows—but there was no mention of the rents from the orchard anywhere in Sir Kunibert's nearly empty accounts book. I sharpened my pen, dipped it into my inkhorn, and began to write out the details of the rent.

The scratch of my quill across the parchment was the only noise other than the crackle of the fire. I was alone with my thoughts for the first time in . . . ever. Solitude and silence. For a moment, I let myself pretend that I wasn't working on accounts underneath the staring gaze of desiccated dragons.

Instead, I pretended I was writing a book.

Whenever I had to copy something or write a letter for my mother, I'd pretend the same thing. I hated the fact that the most exciting employment of my skills was copying numbers or writing down what other people said. Even my push to copy something for the emperor had stuck me with copying a book about horses—me, who was forbidden from riding and deathly afraid of them to boot.

What I really wanted was to write my own book.

Not just a commentary on someone else's work, either. I wanted to write something important. Something that rivaled the works of the heathen philosophers or the great Boethius.

Father Ripertus had taught me the methods of the scribes by having me copy from Boethius's *Consolation of Philosophy*. I hadn't understood any of it when I was younger, but it hadn't given me less of a puff of pride when people asked what I was copying and I could tell them.

Eventually, I stopped caring if I copied great works; I wanted to *make* great works. Certainly, I had a place in the world as the Princess of Alder Brook—the Splayfooted Princess of Alder Brook, as it happened. Every time my mother held court, I could see people watching me, watching my foot and the way I walked; I could see the way their faces were skeptical when I spoke until the sense of my words came through to them. But wouldn't it be nice for people to appreciate the sense of my words and *not* be thinking about the shape of my foot at the same time? Wouldn't it be nice to be remembered for something other than being the little lame princess whose parents never managed to beget a proper heir?

I often thought that writing a book would be the key. Boethius himself had been a favorite of emperors before his downfall; but when people thought of him today, they didn't think of his treason or his time in prison. They thought only of his books on music, arithmetic, geometry, and philosophy.

The problem was, I didn't know what sort of subject I should pursue for such a book. All I knew, really, was about housing and clothing servants, vassals, and tenants; reading land contracts; flattering higher lords through fawning letters; and collecting rents. These were hardly subjects that inspired a flurry of copying or commentary from scholars and scribes. And they were boring.

Pen poised over parchment, I closed my eyes and listened to the blessed silence of the hall. The few servants were all out in the kitchen, preparing for dinner.

This is what it could be like. In my mind's eye, I saw a quiet cloister scriptorium around me, where my fellow nuns copied books while I worked on something else, something greater. The others cast me sideways glances, wishing to know what wondrous thoughts flowed from my pen, but dared not interrupt. A young nun mixed ink for me. And another supplied a steady stream of sharpened pens.

Mathilda of Alder Brook would cease to mean the ruler of a principality that couldn't even afford to buy a professionally scribed copy of *On Horsemanship* for the emperor. Mathilda would become a name coupled with Aristotle and Augustine. Scholars would pore for countless hours over my words, writing fevered glosses in the margins. No one would again equate my name with the evil eye or suggest my mother had walked over a grave while she was pregnant with me.

A cough interrupted the silence of my imaginary cloister.

I opened my eyes to find Lord Parzifal of Hare Hedge staring down at me.

I muffled a scream of surprise so well that it just came out as a strangled squeak. I hadn't seen Parz in weeks. Last time, his hair had tumbled to his shoulders. Now his head was close-cropped, covered in golden stubble.

Even without hair, he was drastically handsome. The first time I'd seen Parz, my head had felt as dense and warm as a cake just out of the oven. I was pleased to note that my head felt no worse than well-cooled yeast bread now. A vast improvement.

"What happened to your hair?" I blurted, then jerked my chin down, angry with myself for being so unmannered. All right, perhaps I was not a *well-cooled* yeast bread at all.

Parz's hand went up to finger the stubble on his scalp—and farther back. He half turned to show me: a brutal-looking wound in some stage between scab and scar, surrounded by an every-colored bruise that went from dull mulberry at the center to pale pear at the edges.

I winced. "What happened?"

"I was . . . too slow on the quintain," he said. I must have looked confused, because he said, "You know that spinning thing you see in training yards? Looks like a scarecrow with a shield attached to one side? You hit the shield with your lance, and if you do it right, when it spins around, it *doesn't* hit you with a bag of sand as you ride past."

I frowned. I knew what a quintain was, but I still didn't understand. "Even if you didn't do it right, a bag of sand shouldn't—" I gestured at my head.

Parz's mouth hardened. "Not only didn't I do it right, but some fatherless donkey weighted the bag with rocks instead of sand. As a prank, I guess, but it was less funny when the bag knocked me out."

"That's horrible! Who would do such a thing?"

"Another squire, visiting with his lord. I guess he grew . . . bored."

"Are you all right?"

"Oh, sure," Parz said. "I only vomited twice, and that was days ago. The barber said more vomiting would be a bad sign. And I didn't break my skull."

"I hope the other squire was punished!"

Parz seated himself on the bench across from me.

"No! That's just it. I was too busy vomiting to explain what happened, and by the time I was done, that pig-hound had swapped out his rocks for sand again, and then he was gone home. No one believes me. They all just think I'm incompetent. A fool."

"But you were hurt!"

"Sir Kunibert doesn't tolerate excuses, not even for a claked head. Not even for an illegal bag of rocks that no one can prove. He's sending me home as soon as I can ride without further injury. It's the end of my training here."

"That's unfair!"

Parz cracked a half smile. "I *was* awfully slow on the quintain." His smile faded. "And I should have noticed that the quintain was weighted wrong, and the way that idiot was clutching his belly and laughing."

"Oh, Parz," I said, and fell silent. Parz leaving Boar House was . . . was a disaster. I didn't travel, and when he went away, I'd never see him again.

The first time I'd met Parz, Sir Kunibert had brought him along to Alder Brook on a visit to my mother. Parz had heard about me and my interest in books, I guess, because he hadn't been in the keep ten minutes before he cornered me and demanded to know where the books on dragons were kept.

You might think I would hate a guest who came up to me and demanded something from me, seemingly at random, and I did try to hate him for a little bit. But Parz had become instantly charming—bowing over my hand, calling me "the princess-librarian," and otherwise using his looks to maximum effect.

I'd been suspicious at first. Hadn't I always, always hated being judged on my appearance? And here I was, letting a boy I didn't know behave brashly to me just because he was pretty to look at?

But there was more to Parz than his face. He was lively and enthusiastic—but he was also kind. We spent an hour talking about dragons before Sir Kunibert finished his business with my mother, claimed his squire, and returned to Boar House.

When Parz had departed, the room and the whole world seemed darker. And now the world would stay that dark, always, once he left Boar House.

I took several deep breaths, trying to screw up my courage to tell Parz how much I was going to miss him.

But he wasn't even looking at me. He was staring at the dragon heads on the wall. "What I need to do," he said thoughtfully, "is to slay a dragon. Yes. And as soon as possible."

chapter 3

"SLAY A DRAGON? WHY?"

"To restore my honor," Parz said. "To prove that I'm more than just an idiot who gets knocked off a horse and put near death by a prank. To prove . . . I'm worth training."

"So!" Judith said angrily. Parz and I both jumped. "In order to train further with a dragon slayer, all you have to do is kill a dragon?" She thunked a mug of hot honey water down in front of me. "Makes *no* sense, Parz. Sounds like a good way to get yourself killed, in fact."

"Judith!" I said, shocked that she would not only interrupt Lord Parzifal and scold him, but that she would also address him so familiarly.

It obviously shocked her, too, because she stared at me, blood draining from her face. "I'm—sorry, Princess Mathilda," she said. "I forgot my—my place."

"I think your apology goes to Lord Parzifal more than me."

"I apologize, Lord Parzifal."

Parz looked from Judith to me and back again. "Um," he said, and finally turned to me. "Tilda, you know things. Where can we find a dragon? A little one?"

Still thrown off by Judith's behavior, I said, "My steward says there's a new dragon at Mount Lorelei."

"I've heard of that one. It's way too big for me to try on my own," Parz said. He didn't look at me as he spoke. He looked at Judith instead.

I glanced at Judith, who met Parz's gaze with a grim mouth and a sharp headshake.

Puzzled, and also slightly embarrassed for some reason, I turned my attention back to the box of contracts before me. The next one I pulled out was a contract for killing a dragon somewhere down the Rhine past Snail Castle.

"There's a record of Sir Kunibert's past dragon slayings in here," I said. "Maybe . . . maybe there's some sort of indication of survivor dragons, or, um, incomplete contracts?"

Parz's eyes lit up, and he nodded.

"So, let's go through all the contracts," I said. "Put them into piles based on what they are. Even if we don't find what we're looking for, it'll help me." I glanced at Judith, who was now being strangely silent and prim. "You too, Judith."

She nodded, and sat down next to me, untangling a few contract ribbons before opening the first one.

"I didn't know you could read," Parz said to Judith.

She was a slow, painstaking reader. Every day, as soon as my lesson with Father Ripertus was over, I had turned around and taught Judith all the letters and words I'd just learned. But her opportunities to practice had been far fewer than mine. Nonetheless, she *could* read and write, even if she had to say everything aloud under her breath as she went.

"There's a lot you don't know about me," Judith muttered.

"Judith!" I said, shocked at her continuance of overfamiliar behavior.

"It's all right, Tilda," Parz said.

I frowned at Parz, wanting to give him an icy scolding about interfering with my servant, but I held my tongue, too confused to know who to blame. I went back to the contracts.

With Parz and Judith to help, I had the contracts sorted into three piles in short order. The first pile was dragon slaying contracts, which Parz now perused eagerly. The second pile was other kinds of income for Sir Kunibert, like his orchard benefice. The third pile was contracts for which Sir Kunibert owed money or service. There was also a small fourth pile of half-heartedly started account books, whose ledgers never went much past the first page.

"Is that everything?" Parz asked.

"Not quite," I said, reaching into the box and pulling out a pale leather book of a size that fitted perfectly to my hand. The binding was limp, and the book moved gently back and forth in a pleasing, flippy way. I unhooked the toggle holding the book closed and opened the fore-edge flap.

The text block of the book was made of thin vellum and it was entirely blank.

"Anything in there?" Parz asked.

I clutched the book to my chest, almost involuntarily. "It's empty," I said, and forced myself to show him the book.

He glanced at it, then continued to study the dragon slaying contracts.

I went through the book more carefully, but it truly was empty. And of such high quality, filled with the perfect vellum.

A door swung open at the far end of the hall. A number of tired-looking young men and boys trooped in, heading for the tables. Parz stood quickly—and just like that, he disappeared out the other door, leaving his stack of contracts behind. I blinked. Judith shrugged.

A half dozen servants swarmed in from the kitchen a moment later, carrying trenchers and platters of meat. Judith hurried to sweep books and contracts into a box, while I more carefully packed up my writing implements. I snatched the blank handbook from her before she could clear it away.

Sir Kunibert emerged from the throng and sat down opposite me to ask how the accounts were going. "I'm still working through the contracts," I said.

"Of course, of course."

"And I found this," I said, handing him the blank book.

He skimmed through the empty pages, a puzzled expression on his face. "I think someone gave me this as bonus payment for dispatching a particularly nasty nest of drakes." He looked up at me. "You like books, don't you?"

"Yes," I said simply.

"You want this one? There are no words in it, but maybe it could be a little payment for your help here."

My mother, had she been home and let me come, would have made it clear that my duties at Boar House today were charitable, and that there would be no reward for them. Nor should I expect any. Nor ask for any. Nor accept any, if offered.

But Mother wasn't at home. Mother—I started guiltily with the realization that this was the first time I'd really thought about her since stepping through the door of Boar House—was lying in Castle Larkspur for the next two months with a bonesetter's cast on her leg.

"Yes," I said, and took the book back. "Thank you," I added after my yes hung between us for a long moment.

Fortunately, Sir Kunibert was a stranger to courtly airs and graces and didn't notice my lapse of manners. He just grunted and thrust his wine cup at a passing servant.

I picked up the lovely hand-sized book that was now mine and caressed its cover. I ran my fingertips over the soft, cut edges of its pages. Then I cracked it open and smelled the unique, faint aroma of all that soft, butter-white vellum just waiting for words.

What was I going to write in it?

I closed the book, stroked the cover again, and put it beside me on the bench, finally turning my attention to the meal.

"WHAT ARE YOU GOING to do with your book?" Judith asked before we climbed into the pleasantly fumigated and aired bed she'd worked on that afternoon.

"I don't know," I said, placing the book under my pillow. I hesitated, wanting to tell her all the other things that had happened at Alder Brook before we left, like my mother's attempt to betroth me to my cousin Ivo; wanting to tell her how much time I spent dreaming of freedom from Alder Brook's responsibilities and rumors and of writing alone in a cloister; wanting to ask about the way she had behaved with Parz earlier. But she yawned hugely, and I yawned hugely . . . and I was keenly aware that Sir Kunibert's female servants were lying on pallets just a few feet away.

It could wait until we had some privacy, I decided.

As tired as I was, I found it difficult to slip into sleep. I lay awake, thinking about my mother laid up at Larkspur. I should write my mother a letter. I began composing it in my head, but every time I got past the greeting, I remembered Parz was leaving Boar House. My thoughts drifted instead to how I should say farewell to him. His friendship had meant so much to me, this boy who wanted to know all about books I'd read (as long as they contained dragons) and cared not in the least that I was a princess and a splayfoot.

But how could I know if my friendship meant anything to *him*? He was a year older than me, and certainly he was kind to me. But he was kind to everyone, it seemed, so what did that signify?

I listened to the strange breathing patterns from

across the room, staring at the flickering patterns of firelight on the walls, while my thoughts ran in circles.

I knew that if I stayed in the room, I'd awaken my companions. I slid from the bed. I told myself I needed the privy, though I could have used the night pot. I just wanted out of the dark, close room. Judith had laid out my sable dressing gown and rabbit-fur slippers for the morning, and I gratefully donned both. Winter's chill was already settling into Boar House's stones.

I crept from the room, crutch scraping flagstones clumsily in the dark. I winced and waited, but no one seemed to awaken.

I let myself out into the darkness of the hall. But my feet didn't carry me on to the privies. I stood at the threshold, watching the still, sleeping lumps of Sir Kunibert's trainees and the male servants clustered around the hearths.

In summer, retainers like these found more privacy by sleeping goodness knew where, but when the cold came, they made do with their friends' elbows and farts and bad breath all night long. As for me, summer or winter, I always shared a bed with my mother and our handmaidens. I stared at the sleepers with bitter jealousy. Winter was on the doorstep, but in a few short months, they could sleep under the stars if they wanted.

"*Hsst,* Tilda."

I almost jumped out of my skin. I looked around to find a shadowed figure on the floor, a silhouette against emberlight. It was Parz, leaning on his elbow and watching me.

I waved slightly and was glad for darkness to cover my blush.

He climbed to his feet and came closer. "Can't sleep?" he asked in a voice just below a whisper.

"No."

He beckoned to me, and together we went outside into the restless autumn night. Dying leaves rattled in trees and skirled on the ground, and the chill air held the tang of woodsmoke and leaf mold. I shivered. I had no love for autumn winds; they made me think of the Wild Hunt, and elves, and all manner of unsavory and fey creatures.

But there was no way I was confessing that to Parz.

We stood shoulder to shoulder, watching the stars and the nearly full moon, and the clouds that dimmed them from time to time. We did not talk, until I blurted out, "I'll miss you, Parz."

I could see his eyes turn toward me by their gleam in the moonlight. His teeth flashed briefly as he smiled. "I'll miss you, too, princess librarian."

I suppressed a giggle. "You know I hate being called that," I said, though that was a lie. I *loved* being called that.

"I know," Parz said. I hoped that was also a lie.

We watched the moonlit clouds gather for rain. We didn't say anything more, even when we turned and went inside. It wasn't the farewell I might have wished for—but I would remember it always.

THE NEXT DAY DAWNED bright. I copied from *On Horsemanship* for a while, and then I continued working on Sir Kunibert's accounts. It was easy to get through all of it without the constant interruptions of Alder Brook, and when I finished just before the midday meal, I stretched luxuriously, feeling unusually satisfied with the day's work. It had all been so simple—just me and the parchment and the pen.

I didn't see Parz all day, but over morning bread and porridge I had eavesdropped intently on two of Kunibert's other squires speaking in low tones about Parz's disgrace. Unfortunately, I didn't learn anything new—other than that Parz was in no way inflating Sir Kunibert's bad opinion of him, and he was definitely leaving soon.

Everyone flooded into the hall to eat dinner, and I didn't say a word to Judith about having finished the accounts. I was wondering what I could write in the blank book, since I could conceivably spend a glorious, uninterrupted afternoon working on it before having to return to the concerns of Alder Brook.

The only problem was, I didn't know what to write.

I was just about to dig into a dish of boar in sour and sweet sauces when a servant tapped Sir Kunibert on his shoulder, then leaned to whisper in his ear. Sir Kunibert looked up at me, a lump of half-chewed meat bulging in his cheek. "Your cousin is here."

I frowned in confusion. "My cousin is here," I repeated, trying to understand.

Sir Kunibert shrugged. "That's what I've been told. He wants to speak with you, in private—I guess he's in the courtyard."

He. I had only one male cousin, the son of the lord of Larkspur, where my mother had been injured. Why would anyone come all the way from Larkspur unless there was bad news? Why would he come on to Boar House from Alder Brook, unless the news was *very* bad?

I got to my feet, looking around frantically for Judith. I couldn't spot her—she must have been fetching something from the kitchen.

Heart in my throat, I grabbed my crutch and hurried outside alone.

Cousin Ivo stood in the courtyard, the autumn sunlight turning his pale hair even brighter. He wore his sparse beard combed into five ridiculous points.

He raked me with a glance. "Hello, Mathilda. Still a cripple, I see."

chapter 4

I FLINCHED, THEN IMMEDIATELY HATED MYSELF FOR flinching. That word shouldn't matter to me. No such words should matter to me.

But they did.

"If you traveled all this way to insult me, Ivo, you could have spared yourself the trip."

"No, I didn't come all this way *just* to insult you," Ivo said. "I've come to take Alder Brook from you."

I stared at Ivo, dumbfounded—and then I laughed. I didn't believe him. Take Alder Brook from me? How could he *take* Alder Brook from me? My mother would never allow it.

"I thought you were coming to tell me something bad happened to my mother," I said, still laughing.

Ivo's eyes narrowed. "Something bad *did* happen to your mother," he said ominously, and there was suddenly a blade in his hand, a mean little dagger. "Her leg is broken."

I stopped laughing as I suddenly realized: She wasn't recuperating at Larkspur. She was imprisoned there. For the first time since I'd heard she was following physician's orders to stay in bed for two months, the world made sense again.

"Come quietly, and you won't get hurt too," Ivo said, grabbing my arm.

"What did you do to my mother?" In shock, I let him propel me away from Boar House and down toward the river. I looked all around for help, but everyone was inside eating or serving dinner.

"She had an *accident*." The way he said the word told me it had been no accident.

I opened my mouth to yell or scream, but before I could even draw my breath all the way, there was a sharpness digging into my ribs. I exhaled in a small squeak.

"I said to come *quietly*," Ivo growled.

"Where are you taking me?" I asked, trying to move my ribs away from Ivo's knife.

"I have an ideal prison for you downriver."

Imprisonment, then, not murder. "And my mother?"

"She's also my prisoner. She'll remain with my parents at Larkspur until after Christmas Day."

"Why Christmas Day?"

Ivo spoke slowly, as to a simpleton. "When Christmas Day comes and you are not at Alder Brook to receive the rents and hear the reswearing of your vassals' oaths, I will simply step in and become Prince of Alder Brook in your place."

"As simple as that!"

"You don't believe me." Ivo smiled, and jerked my arm a little, so that I stumbled against him. "You know what they call you, don't you? The Splayfooted Princess. The Pigeon-toed Princess. Mathilda the Gravefoot. And those are just the people *laughing* at you."

I looked at my twice-twisted foot: one twist pointed my toes inward at my other foot, which they call being pigeon-toed, and the second twist turned my foot over so that I walked on the outside edge, which they call being splayfooted.

I'd heard the names whispered behind my back all my life. I'd often wanted to show the whisperers the horrible ulcers that came from walking too much, and watch them run screaming. But of course, princesses do not do such things.

"Get in the boat," Ivo said. I shook my head, coming out of my stupor to see that we had reached the riverbank. I cast one last look back at Boar House, but it was shut up tight; everyone was inside, eating and laughing. Upstream, Alder Brook presented an impassive wall to the river. I could see no figures in the distance, no sign of any activity. It was dinnertime there, too.

I crawled into the boat and wondered: How had Ivo known where to find me? He had to have gone to Alder Brook first. They had to have sent him down here to Boar House alone. Why would anyone have done that? Unless . . . unless they understood his mission and wanted him to succeed.

I blinked hard for a moment, trying to keep my vision clear. I'd spent a lot of my life swallowing sobs and hiding tears; so today was like all those other days. Practice made perfect.

"Can you swim?" Ivo asked, and then scoffed: "Like I'd believe what you said, anyway." He pulled out a small length of rope and tied my hands with it. I stared at my bound wrists, astonished.

"Why not just kill me?" I finally asked.

Ivo clambered into the boat and cast off. "Really? Is that what you think of me, Tilda?"

"You *are* usurping my principality," I said.

"Murder is a terrible sin." He shipped the oars and rowed out into the current. "Plus my mother said not to kill you, in case we need you later. And my father says you're the perfect hostage to keep your mother in line."

"So, your whole family is helping out with stealing Alder Brook. That's nice. And how, exactly, are you going to convince Alder Brook to just let you take over?"

Ivo rested on his oars, and smiled. "My sources assure me it won't be a problem."

"Your sources?"

"They say your mother walked over a grave when she carried you. They say you bring bad luck and death. They say your father died because of you, or because of some sin in his past, the same sin that caused your gravefoot. They say that if even some desperate knight could be convinced to marry you, he'd die before the first year was out, because there's a devil's mark on you. *Everyone* knows you're cursed, Tilda."

Everyone? He had to be exaggerating. But then I thought about Aged Arnolt refusing to speak to me, and the servant girl Roswitha making the sign against the evil eye, and the game the children played that mocked my limp.

I felt like Ivo had punched me in the belly. It was true that Alder Brook was in a delicate place, monetarily speaking, but that was far from cursed. We watched every silver pfennig and gold mark and couldn't afford to lose two cows to a dragon, as Horrible had pointed out. I knew the accounts as well as anyone. Things had been hard since Alder Brook had lost its prince, my father, while he was on pilgrimage to free the Holy Land.

After he'd died, we'd had to give a large sum of money to the emperor instead of sending our knights to him for military service. If we had kept the money and sent the knights, we would have been invaded by one of our ambitious neighbors. Alder Brook might be the smallest of the empire's principalities, but it was still a ripe plum, being a freehold, owing nothing to anyone except the emperor.

And everyone—my vassals, my servants, my tenants—thought that I was cursed? That Alder Brook was cursed? That *we* were cursed?

That was what Horrible and Father Ripertus had been talking about before I interrupted them. "The rumors do not help," Father Ripertus had said when my mother couldn't make a betrothal for me. The rumors were about the curse.

I thought about Horrible and how he'd been so easy to convince to let me come downstream to Boar House, away from Alder Brook and the few people who might protect me. Ivo had allies on the inside. What if Horrible had known all along what was going to happen to my mother at Larkspur? Had he known when he let me go to Sir Kunibert that he'd never have to deal with me again?

Who else might have conspired with Ivo? Who else might cheer when they heard I was gone? The signs, the games, the rumors, the stares I'd received since my earliest years . . . perhaps the question was who *wouldn't* cheer?

I felt the ice mask descend on my face, and the bands of iron wrap around my heart once more. Alder Brook didn't love me, and I didn't love them. If they truly didn't want me to be their princess . . .

"You can have it," I said dully.

I'd caught him off guard. "What?"

I swallowed against the weird lump in my throat—part anger, part a hundred other feelings I couldn't even name. "Yes. Alder Brook is yours. They hate me. They think I'm cursed. . . . So. Take it."

I'd surprised him. His mouth was a perfect O of frozen amazement. Then his bloodless lips twisted into a grin. "Nice try, Tilda. Did you think I'd buy that speech and just let you go?"

But I was already thinking about where I *could* go. Where I *wanted* to go. I could go to a cloister and become a nun. I could write books all day, every day. And Ivo could have Alder Brook and its malcontents, its sly sign makers and its mockers. Ivo could have the prison.

I could be free.

"You couldn't possibly think that would work," Ivo continued, and steered the boat closer to the center of the current. "I mean . . . I trust you about as far as you can run."

I glared at him. "It's one thing to steal my lands, Ivo. It's another thing to insult me for deformities of my body that I cannot control."

"Don't be a child," Ivo said. "Words don't hurt. Say whatever you like about me, and I shall smile and smile!"

"Maybe you just don't understand what people are saying."

His eyes shifted up and right, then returned to me. My words still hadn't sunk in. "All right. Here's how it's going to work: I'm going to imprison you at Snail Castle until after Christmas Day and the New Year."

"And then what?"

"And then I'll marry you off as I see fit, as your overlord," he said. "And instead of giving a dowry for you, I'll command a bride-price."

I raised an eyebrow. "I'm thirteen. You aren't going to be able to marry me off for a while."

"That might be true if I cared a jot for your happiness." He steered us around a fallen tree. "I don't, just to clarify."

"Your father wouldn't agree to have you marry

me, I heard—what makes you think anyone else will agree to it?"

"You're still one of the Illustrious," Ivo said. Illustrious was my rank, a title reserved for families like mine, born both free and landed. While even the free owed some service to the emperor, unfree families of great wealth and power were at the beck and call of their liege lord, and they did not truly own their lands. The service of unfree families could even be traded away to other lords.

Children claimed the free or unfree status of their mothers, no matter how property and titles were inherited. "There are any number of wealthy unfree knights, Tilda, who would pay well to have freeborn children and a princely ally with the emperor's ear."

I choked on a laugh. The emperor's ear? He thought he could leverage becoming Prince of Alder Brook into advising the emperor? With what money, what wit, and what charm?

Ivo had no understanding of how far Alder Brook was from the emperor's court. Not in distance, but in influence. Even with two counts and nine knights in service to Alder Brook, we worried too much, day to day, about the fodder of dairy cattle to consider empire building. Court life bankrupted places with more money than Alder Brook. I might be a princess, but there were dukes and counts wealthier and more powerful than me, and they were all at court throwing around their money to curry favor.

I couldn't believe Horrible Hermannus would support this idiot, but then again, I hadn't nicknamed him Horrible for nothing.

"Can't I just join a cloister after all of this is over?"

He snorted. "Entering a cloister takes a pretty pfennig. How would you afford that? Alder Brook and all its properties belong to me now, and I'm not paying your dowry to the Church."

"But I'm *letting* you have Alder Brook!"

"Oh, heavens, I don't believe that. Do you think I've never heard of subterfuge, little girl?"

Normally, with an opening like that, I would have held my tongue; a princess does not mock those of lesser ability and intelligence. But Ivo was a true villain.

"I'm surprised you know such a big word for 'lying and playacting,'" I said.

He leaned forward and slapped my face. I clenched my teeth to keep from crying out. But I couldn't help but smile a little bit too. Words didn't hurt? Then why punish me when I said hurtful words?

"Why won't you believe I'm not going to make trouble for you in claiming Alder Brook?" I asked, trying to sound innocent.

"You never were a biddable girl; you've never done

what you were told before. Why would you start now?"

"What are you talking about? I always do as I'm told!" I practically shouted, the injustice of this accusation hit me so hard. First this pig-hound broke my mother's leg then, when he stole my lands, refused to believe me when I said he could have them? "All I ever do is what I'm told!" The words tore at my throat, they came out of me with such force. Angry tears streaked down my cheeks.

"Ugh." Ivo whipped a kerchief out of his sleeve, balled it up, and shoved it into my mouth. From the other sleeve came a second kerchief, which he tied into a gag, silencing me. "You *would* cry."

I wished I could tell him to shut up.

WE STOPPED SHY OF the confluence of the Rhine and the Victory Rivers at Snail Castle, whose lord and lady were supposedly in service to Alder Brook, though clearly Ivo now had gained their loyalty. They bowed to Ivo and called him Prince. To me, they still bowed, but did meet my eyes or call me by name.

I had a sour realization: I was now a prisoner, but nothing had really changed since I was their princess. They treated me about as they had when they'd visited Alder Brook in the past. They had refused to look too closely at me then, too—why? In case they could catch splayfootedness through eye contact?

Ivo trailed along behind as I was locked into a high tower room. He grinned at me through the barred window of my door.

"Enjoy your stay, Tilda. I'll enjoy Alder Brook."

"Before you go—you might want to think of what you're going to say to Farmer Everwinus tomorrow. Farmer Wecelo is going to burn the south field, but Everwinus is convinced he has a say over it."

Ivo sneered. "Why are you telling me this? This is what the steward is for." He turned and hurried down the stairs.

"But Sir Hermannus is—" I started to call after him. Horrible Hermannus was cousin to Everwinus. Wecelo wouldn't trust Horrible to be impartial, and Alder Brook would have a feud brewing if the judgment wasn't handled well.

But Ivo didn't want to hear it.

Not very princely of him.

SUPPER WAS LIGHT, BEING little more than warm broth and bread. I was given wood and a fire striker but had to build my fire myself. And then? And then, nothing. I had nothing to do.

I paced my room until my foot ached, which didn't take very long. I stared out the window until it grew dark. Then I sat on the bed.

Boethius's most famous book was written after

he was imprisoned by King Theodoric the Great. I once foolishly told my mother that I was jealous of Boethius's time in prison, to write whatever he wanted without anyone bothering him. Mother had set me to calculating how much cheese we could expect to gain if we bought one, three, and five new cows, and then how much cheese we could expect to lose if we sold one, three, and five old cows. Then the same exercise with goats. It was a punishment for not being grateful for what I had.

I'd felt fairly well punished at the time, but now I really understood how foolish I had been in my jealousy.

I checked the pouch at my waist. Three silver pfennigs. Would that be enough to bribe a servant to bring me pen, ink, and parchment? And if it was enough money . . . would I be able to put aside what was happening, all the worry over my mother, over Alder Brook and my future, all my confusion and despair, and just start writing? I wasn't Boethius.

I thought about my mother lying with her broken leg at Larkspur, held captive by Ivo's vile family. Even while I worried for her, I couldn't believe she'd tried to betroth me to Ivo. She must be as confused and unhappy as me.

The thing was, I had been confused and unhappy before I found myself locked in a small tower room at

Snail Castle. I didn't want to be a princess. What I most wanted was to travel the world and read in all the great libraries and write a book. Freely. Free of accounts and rents and oaths and contracts. Free of needlework, signs against the evil eye, and lectures on duty.

Free of people who thought they knew me, but who really only knew my father's death, my foot, and my empty treasury.

I curled up on the bed and slipped into an unhappy sleep, and only woke when something touched my shoulder. My eyes flew open to find a dark, shadowed figure crouched over me. A firm hand came across my mouth, just in time to stifle my scream.

chapter 5

"PRINCESS! PRINCESS!" A VOICE HISSED IN MY EAR. "Hold! Hold still!"

I was firmly pinned by the stranger's hands, so I shot out a fist to strike at my attacker's throat with all the strength I could muster. I heard a satisfying cry of pain, but the hands did not release me.

"Please hold!" the whisper implored. "It's me! Parz! Judith sent me!"

I stopped struggling. The hand came away from my mouth.

"Parz?" I sat up. "What are you doing here?"

"I'm, um, rescuing you. When I'm not getting punched in the throat."

I made a weird noise, somewhere between a gasp

and a laugh, and almost gave myself hiccups because of it. I hadn't looked for rescue. I hadn't even *dreamed* of rescue.

"We have to stay quiet," Parz said. "Are you ready to go?"

I hadn't taken off my clothes to sleep, because I'd been afraid my wardens might steal them in the night. "I'm ready."

"May I lend you my arm?" he whispered.

I no more wanted Parz's help than I wanted to be helpless. I didn't want him—or anyone—to see me as weak. My parents always thought me fragile, and it was true that I'd suffered from many sores and infections on my foot, as well as the other pains by walking in such a wretched manner, and that I could not go very far, very fast, unaided. But what I lacked in speed and stamina and general well-being, I tried to make up for in every other way. Stubbornness was sometimes all I had.

But now was not the time for stubbornness, now was the time for speed. I pulled my crutch from under the bed and took Parz's arm.

We crept down the stairs with inexpert stealth, and stopped at the edge of Snail Castle's great hall. We listened to the noises of the room for a long moment, checking for movement among the sleeping retainers. But no one had seriously entertained the notion I might escape, or that a rescue might be mounted, and not a soul saw us leave.

Parz lifted the bar on the door with a struggle that made too much noise and yet woke no one. He led me from the sleeping hall, out into the night.

Snail Castle was just a keep on a hill, with no real outer perimeter. Parz led me easily off into a copse of trees some distance on. A small pool of lamplight awaited us in a clearing. As we approached, a cloaked figure strode from the shadows and dramatically threw back his hood.

Well. *Her* hood. It was Judith.

We rushed to embrace. "You're all right?" she asked, looking me over.

"I'm fine now!" I said, and shivered in the chill air.

"You're cold!" She scurried behind a tree and pulled out our clothes chest. From it she drew my cloak and swung it around my shoulders.

"Thank you," I said. "Thanks to you both! How did you find me?"

"You have Parz to thank—he saw you going off with Ivo from the upper floor of Boar House—"

"I didn't realize until too late that you were being kidnapped," Parz said sheepishly.

"He came to get me, and we followed Ivo down here to Snail Castle. What happened? What is Ivo *doing*?"

I laughed without mirth, and told them all about Ivo's imprisonment of my mother and his plan to take over Alder Brook. "If I don't turn up to collect the rents and hear the renewed oaths of fealty on Christmas Day, then I forfeit my claim on Alder Brook to Ivo."

Judith shook her head. "He's an idiot! No one is going to stand for that. Are you ready to go?"

"Go where?"

"Back to reclaim Alder Brook!" Judith said.

"Oh!" I said, and stared at Judith, startled to realize that I did not want to return to Alder Brook. I hadn't been trying to fool Cousin Ivo; I hadn't been trying to make the best of a bad situation. I really did not want to go back.

I had no idea how to explain that to Judith.

"It's too soon," Parz said, and I turned to him gratefully. "Ivo will just devise another plan. He still has your mother."

"Right!" I said eagerly. "Also, Ivo has at least one spy—maybe dozens—inside Alder Brook."

"Who?" Judith said, her voice rising on an indignant note. Alarmed, Parz and I both shushed Judith, looking back toward Snail Castle's dark shape.

"We need to get away from here, whatever we do," Parz said, disappearing among the trees. He returned moments later leading out an enormous warhorse. I immediately hid behind Judith.

Parz laughed. "What are you doing, Tilda?"

I didn't want to say I was afraid of the horse. But I was. I peered at it over Judith's shoulder.

"I was never taught to ride," I said.

Judith said, "In fact, she was never *allowed* to ride."

"Why?" Parz asked.

"My foot," I said, after a bare moment's hesitation. "The position of my foot won't allow it."

"Won't it? You could ride aside instead of astride."

"And it's dangerous," I blurted out. My mother had assured me that if a horse stepped on my foot, or threw me, I would walk with an even worse limp than the one I already possessed, or stop walking altogether. I had always stayed well away from the stables.

"Don't worry, I'll ride with you," Parz said.

Judith gave me a gentle pat on the shoulder as she dragged our clothes chest into the trees.

She returned on the back of a dangerous-looking palfrey that puffed and snorted and danced around. I stared, too surprised to be frightened. When had Judith learned to ride?

She knocked on the clothes chest mounted behind her. "All set," she said.

"Time to go," Parz said, snagging me around the waist. He threw me onto the warhorse before I had a chance to protest. I clutched. I couldn't say *what* I clutched, since my eyes were closed, but I think I got some mane and some saddle.

"Open your eyes," Parz said, climbing up behind me. I peeked out from behind my eyelids and closed them again immediately.

I was too far from the ground. My feet dangled pointlessly from where I perched sideways before Parz. He held me loosely around the waist, but I wasn't sure that would be enough to keep me from slipping off.

We hurried away from Snail Castle, and I held on to the saddle for dear life and wished Parz would hold me more tightly. And not because he was handsome and noble and brave, but because I didn't want to die like this.

In fact, I wanted to like riding with Parz much more than I actually did, even after the galloping was over and we slowed to a walk. I felt sure I was supposed to enjoy being half embraced by him. But mostly, fear subsided into the dull acceptance that, actually, riding a horse was just a little bit more about discomfort than terror. My feet got cold, my sit-bones got sore, and I found that I did not like Parz's onion breath in my ear.

Every time I glanced over at Judith, she was looking like she reveled in the moment; but then, she wasn't smelling onions.

Our steeds sent up plumes of white breath into

the starlit night. Distant smokehouses curing the autumn's pork scented the air and reminded me of Alder Brook. I yawned hugely, and longed for a fire and the comfort of my mother's sea-duck-down blankets.

Judith trotted up alongside us when the road widened.

"You're sure someone inside Alder Brook is working for Ivo?" she asked.

"How else would Ivo know to come find me at Boar House?" I said. "Why else would he think his plan would succeed?"

"He could have bribed someone," Judith said.

"Or worse," Parz said. "He might've threatened violence."

"Alder Brook will never side with him over Tilda!" Judith said stoutly.

I didn't know about that. Nothing that had happened recently made me think that the people of Alder Brook wouldn't let Ivo put me in the dungeon, or ship me off to the dragon at Mount Lorelei, for all I knew. When they saw strong young Ivo with his two good feet and a face that could catch a rich bride easily enough, they wouldn't care if he fanned feuds between Everwinus and Wecelo or whoever. It would be better for everyone in the long run, and they would see it that way.

"I don't think I can return to Alder Brook without my mother," I hedged.

"So . . . ," Judith said. "We should rescue your mother."

"I don't want to say that's impossible," Parz said. "But we don't exactly have an army."

"You rescued Tilda from Snail Castle—snatched her right from under their noses!"

"Snail Castle is tiny and unfortified, and I'd been there before. We only had to rescue Tilda, and she can walk. Princess Isobel's leg is broken, and she has two—three?—ladies-in-waiting with her, at the very least. I've never been to Castle Larkspur, but from all I've heard, it's nearly as well defended as Alder Brook Keep. Now, listen. I've been thinking. You both can come with me until it's time to reclaim Alder Brook. Ivo won't think to look for you in the places I'm going."

"Where exactly are you going?" I asked.

"Well, I'm not sure *where* yet, but I'm going to hunt down a dragon and kill it," Parz said. "Regain my honor, and prove to Sir Kunibert that I'm a worthy squire."

Judith and I were silent, trying to read each other's faces in the dark and failing miserably.

"You'd be a great help to me," Parz continued.

"I'm not exactly dragon slayer material," I said stiffly.

"You're better than dragon slayer material, Tilda," he said. "I need you."

"You do?"

"Let's be honest. I'm not a real dragon slayer yet. I had years of training ahead of me, and Sir Kunibert was very closemouthed with his information. You remember how we met. . . ."

I sighed and nodded. "You were looking for books on dragons. Alder Brook didn't have any."

"You had more than Sir Kunibert! You had those biographies of saints who slew dragons—and what's more, you read them for me, and told me everything useful in them. Like Patrick tricking the ancient dragon into crawling inside a tree trunk and kicking it into the sea. There have to be more books about dragons, in a cloister somewhere—we can go, and read their books about dragons. I need you—I need the knowledge you can find, to make up for my unfinished training."

An idea struck me. "Too bad I don't have the blank book Sir Kunibert gave me," I said. "I could've used it to record everything we find."

Judith fumbled with a saddlebag. "You mean *this* blank book?" She rode closer and pushed it into my hands.

"Oh, yes!" I hugged the little book to me, stroking its soft leather cover with my thumbs. "Parz, I could write a handbook for you!"

"A handbook for dragon slayers," Parz said, clearly struck by the idea. "We can also go around the countryside looking for the best information on dragon slaying—consult with other dragon slayers, certainly, but also visit places where famous dragons were slain—and you can record it all."

This was it! This was my dream of writing something all my own—something important. It didn't exactly rival the works of the heathen philosophers, but it could be my answer to Aristotle and Xenophon. A handbook for dragon slayers, written by me, Mathilda of Alder Brook.

"And Judith will help me slay the dragon," Parz said.

"Judith will—what?"

Judith was silent. Parz was silent.

"I don't think—" I began.

"Most Illustrious, I have a confession," Judith interrupted.

She rarely called me Most Illustrious, even though it was my proper title. She must be feeling very guilty about something.

Parz interrupted. "It was all my fault, Tilda."

"No," Judith said. "It's mine." She took a deep breath. "I've been sneaking away from Alder Brook to practice with Parz."

"You've been . . . To practice *what* with Parz?"

"Riding a warhorse, throwing spears, the quintain, the sword, the lance. . . ."

"You have? Why?"

Judith made an exasperated sound.

"Because I needed a friend," Parz said quietly. "I've been the least of Sir Kunibert's squires for a long while. My head . . . was only the most recent problem, and it was the drop that caused the cup to run over, but this had been a long time coming. I needed someone to practice with for extra time, where the others couldn't see me. And . . . Judith agreed to."

"I see." I was almost too shocked to speak. I wished that I could see Judith's face, but the starlight was too dim. "Ah!" I said, suddenly putting together the puzzle of Judith's behaviors of the last months. "This is why you got up earlier than everyone else all summer—you weren't in the privies with a bowel complaint at all!"

"Tilda," Judith protested with a moan.

"Oh, no. You don't get to make up a story like that and expect me to not share it with Parz. Oh! And you haven't gotten suddenly clumsier—all your mystery bruises are from these practices?"

"Yes," Judith said.

"And *that* is why you are overly familiar with Lord Parzifal." I snapped my fingers, pleased with how I'd put all the disparate pieces together. “And why you know how to ride a horse.”

“I’ll accept my punishment without complaint,” Judith said, and my satisfaction faded. Judith had kept secrets from me, done things she shouldn’t have done—but she had not in the end abandoned her duty to Alder Brook. And right now, I was keeping a secret from her, one far bigger. I couldn’t tell her—couldn’t bring myself to tell her—that I wanted no part of Alder Brook anymore.

“Tilda? Are you all right?” Judith asked.

“I’m fine. There’s no punishment, Judith,” I said. “I couldn’t punish you for helping Parz, even if it would be right and proper.”

“Thank you, Tilda,” Judith said. She was relieved, of course, but I could hear her eagerness. She wanted to do this, she wanted to slay dragons with Parz.

It was base deceit, on my part, to use her secret wishes to aid my own. If I agreed to this plan, the promise of dragon slaying would keep her distracted from our return to Alder Brook for quite some time.

I nodded. “So it’s settled, then? We’re going to become dragon slayers.”

chapter 6

WE MOVED ON THROUGH THE NIGHT, ANXIOUS TO leave Snail Castle far behind. The autumn winds had stilled, which was a relief; the last thing we needed was the threat of the Wild Hunt and their windstorm sweeping down on us.

To keep ourselves awake, we talked about dragons and the handbook for dragon slayers. Or rather, the *Handbook for Dragon Slayers*—that was clearly the book's title. My fingers twitched, yearning for quills and ink. I wanted to take notes. I bent my fingers to hold an imaginary pen and traced the opening words on my leg. I would begin with a curse—a book curse, to protect the *Handbook*.

We shared everything we knew about dragons,

whether we thought the others might know it or not. I told the stories of Saint Magnus Dragonslayer that I had looked up for Parz. The town of River Bend—but two days' ride up the Rhine from here—had been haunted by dragons until Saint Magnus and his friend Theodor came to drive them out. Saint Magnus had commanded the chief of the dragons to hold still, and smashed in its skull with his holy staff.

"It's too bad none of us are more holy," I said. "That seems to be the most effective way to kill dragons."

"I don't have a staff, anyway," Parz said. "We may have to go a different route."

"Saint Magnus also killed a dragon at Horsehead Gorge in the south," I said. "When the dragon tried to eat him, he threw resin and pitch into its mouth, which ignited on the dragon's internal fires and burned it from the inside out."

"Now that's a practical tactic!" Parz said. "We should definitely get some resin and pitch."

"Saint Magnus also tamed a tribe of bears and taught them to kill demons," I said.

Parz's voice turned wistful. "Imagine what we could do with a tribe of bears."

"Bears eat a lot, and they're rather testy," Judith said. "Let's leave bear training to the saints."

WE CAME INTO THE town of King's Winter with first light and the tolling of the Matins bells.

Parz reined in and waited for Judith. "Here's the plan. Make it known that we are crossing the Rhine today and heading toward Aix. When we leave town, we'll double back and make sure no one knows where we're really going. That way, if Ivo or anyone tries to follow us, he'll only find a false trail."

"Clever," Judith said.

Parz led the way through town to a small guesthouse. I was grateful to be off the horse for a while. It had ceased to be terrifying, but I felt rather like a sack of salt. Or maybe turnips.

Judith carried our chest with the few belongings she had packed for Boar House, and she and I went up to the room that Parz secured for us. Hot water was brought, and we commenced washing, dressing, and combing.

I looked over my possessions. For clothing, counting what I'd been wearing when I was kidnapped by Ivo, I now owned only two dresses and a fur cloak. I had a little jewelry: a brooch to fasten my mantle, a silver fillet for my head, and a silver girdle for my hips. My purse held only the three pfennigs I had thought to bribe servants with at Snail Castle, for I'd never replenished it after I gave alms at church last. I also had my writing box and the blank book Sir Kunibert had given me.

I'd given up a lot in giving up Alder Brook, but they were only material possessions. I smiled a little, running my finger over soaked-in ink splotches on my writing box. I imagined sitting close to Parz in an empty library, reading together from a book about dragons. I imagined our hands resting side by side as we read from the same book, until our littlest fingers brushed against each other and then linked together.

"I know what you're thinking," Judith said. I looked up, startled, and blushed.

"You do?"

"We'll take back Alder Brook, Princess. Don't you worry. Ivo won't win."

It wasn't what I was thinking, of course, but I'd rather have told her the embarrassing thing about Parz's fingers than that I had no intention of taking back Alder Brook. I let the conversation drop.

We spent less than an hour at the guesthouse, eating quickly after the washup. I didn't look forward to returning to my imitation of a sack of turnips, but at least the horse wasn't as frightening as before. I had no notion of how people could ride such long distances as they did, though; it was sincerely uncomfortable.

We returned to the road, performed Parz's

doubling-back trick, and then stopped to consider where we should go next.

"Saint Disibod's Cloister," I announced. "That's what we should make for. It has the oldest library of anywhere around, without going to a big city or too close to Alder Brook."

Parz looked like he wanted to say something, then just nodded agreeably.

We rode with the great Rhine River to our right and vineyard-covered mountains on our left.

"Drachenfels," Parz said with a sigh in my ear. He had, thankfully, cleaned his teeth and gotten a sprig of mint at some point, and was much less oniony.

"Pardon?"

"That mountain is Drachenfels—the dragon cliff—where the hero Siegfried slew Fafnir the dragon."

I looked at the mountain covered in autumn-bright trees, at the vintners harvesting grapes at its foot. That was Drachenfels? I had no notion it was so close to Alder Brook.

"We should put Siegfried's story in the *Handbook*," I said.

"I know that one by heart," Parz said.

"You do?"

"Certainly. My greatfather used to tell it to me. There is a lot of it I don't remember very well, about how Fafnir stole a king's treasury and took it up there to Drachenfels to hide it."

"The Rhinegold," I said. I knew this story a little. Parz waved away the importance of gold and went on.

"Siegfried watched the dragon's habits carefully every day, and discovered the path it took down to the water to drink. Siegfried dug a ditch across the dragon's path, and hid in it. And when the dragon passed over him, he stabbed the dragon from below. The blood rained down upon him, and it made his skin invulnerable from that day forward. All but one tiny spot where a linden leaf had fallen, and that, of course, was the spot where one day, much later, someone did stab him, and kill him."

I studied Drachenfels, noting half a dozen paths coming down through the vineyards to the Rhine. Any of them could have been where Siegfried dug his trench and slew Fafnir.

"Do you think all dragon blood makes you invulnerable?" I asked.

"Long ago, perhaps, but our dragons now are smaller than they were in the old days, and less powerful."

We stopped to eat at midday, and talked more about killing dragons. I told them the story of Saint Marthe and the dragon Tarasque, whose breath and teeth were poisoned. Saint Marthe's main weapon against Tarasque in the dark forest of Nerluc was the sign of the cross. When she made the sign, the dragon grew docile and just let her bind him with her girdle, after which the people of Nerluc stabbed the dragon with spears.

"We're still not holy enough for that to work," Judith said. "But it makes sense: Dragons are evil, so holiness is the best way to defeat them."

"And Saint Marthe was holier than most," I said. "Her sister was Mary Magdalene. We need fewer saint stories and more regular dragon slayer stories. Did Sir Kunibert ever tell you about his battles?"

"He always said that practice was far more important than stories," Parz said. "I should tell you, I found resin and pitch for sale in King's Winter."

"Seems a little early to buy resin and pitch," I said. "I haven't even set down a word in the *Handbook* yet."

"Maybe a little early," Parz agreed, and we fell silent for a time.

My head tipped over onto Parz's chest, and—my thoughts confused—I wondered when I would start to feel free and relieved about abandoning Alder Brook to Ivo. I had done the right thing, hadn't I? The people of Alder Brook, from Aged Arnolt to Roswitha, and every tenant farmer, unfree knight, blacksmith, and priest who lived on our lands or owed service to the family would be happier this way. Ivo had two strong legs. No one would look at him and think about curses. No one would wonder if he could attract a good spouse. No one would blame him for my father's death or think he brought misfortune. He wouldn't administer Alder Brook better than I could, but just by being their prince he would make everyone happier.

Including me.

My thoughts circled away from those uncomfortable subjects and drifted to dragon blood and dragon gold, and how I would record Fafnir's story in the *Handbook*. I was still tracing words on my thigh when I fell quite deeply asleep.

I WOKE WHEN THE horse halted.

"Time to stop for the night," Parz said, and bounced to the ground.

"Here?" I asked, looking around me for a sign of a guesthouse or any sort of house at all.

"Here," Parz said firmly, and reached up to swing me down from the horse. I bit my lip against a moan of pain when my stiffened legs caught my weight.

Judith saw my expression and scrambled down from her horse to bring me my crutch.

"Tilda could use a bath and a soft bed," Judith said, giving me her shoulder to lean on.

"No guesthouses," Parz said. "Not overnight,

anyway. Guesthouses mean people who can remember our descriptions and overhear our talk."

Judith raised her voice a little. "You cannot ask a princess to sleep outside!"

I straightened my spine and lifted my chin. "Perhaps, but a princess can *offer* to sleep outside."

Parz's face split into an appreciative grin. I grinned back, but quickly found my way to a rock, and used it to lower myself to the ground, unsteady on my feet.

We made camp near a small rivulet off the Willows River, using leaf litter as bed stuffing and our cloaks for covers. I couldn't help regretting the rest of my warm clothes abandoned at Alder Brook. Like my other two cloaks. Those would have made my outdoor bed somewhat nicer.

Parz took care of the horses while Judith built a fire. I considered our food stores. We had only a quarter wheel of cheese and some bread, until Judith gleaned hazelnuts from a hedge.

The sun set, and we ate. Parz produced a pot of small ale to wash the meal down, though it was unfiltered and as thick as breakfast gruel, so we had to chew it as much as drink it.

My body ached from the day's riding, and my foot ached because it always did, but my belly was full and I was free. I stretched and sighed. I wanted to massage my leg and foot, but I was embarrassed to do so in front of Parz.

Judith saw me flexing my foot and came over to take it in her lap. When I made to pull it back underneath my cloak, she swatted at me lightly. "You're in pain, Tilda."

Parz didn't look up, being busy whittling something.

"What are you so intent on whittling, Parz—I mean, Lord Parzifal?" Judith asked.

"Spears," Parz said. "In case we meet a dragon tomorrow."

Judith quirked her eyebrows at me, and I shrugged. She dug her thumbs into the tight tendons of my foot. I sucked my breath in to keep from crying out. Parz glanced up. I tried not to blush. I probably wouldn't be able to sleep for cramping if Judith didn't help me.

"Calm night," Parz commented a moment later. "A lucky thing for this time of year. We wouldn't want to meet the Wild Hunt."

"Hush!" Judith said. "Don't speak of them."

I laughed uneasily. "The Wild Hunt aren't like hearthgoblins or elves. They can't hear you talking about them from miles away. And even if they could, they don't come when you mention them."

"I still don't want to talk about . . . them," Judith said.

We fell silent, but I doubted any of us stopped thinking of the group of immortal huntsmen who rode with their horses and hounds across the earth on restless nights, collecting souls of the dead and punishing wrongdoers. We'd all heard stories of them when the wind rose in the autumn. *Take care to speak the truth, or the Wild Hunt might find you*, Frau Oda, my mother's handmaiden, used to say to Judith and me.

When Judith was done with my foot, I got up and pulled out my writing box and the *Handbook*. Balancing the book on my lap, I opened to the first page, and wrote out the book curse I had been planning.

"What are you writing, Tilda?" Parz asked.

"The book curse. Every book needs one." I read it out loud. "Whosoever steals this book shall BURN in the FIERY CONFLAGRATION of a DRAGON'S BREATH and will also LOSE THEIR NOSE to PUTREFACTION."

"Ew, putrefacting noses? That's disgusting!" Judith said.

"You can't scare people with a curse if it isn't terrifying," I said.

Parz frowned. "Is it really going to stop anyone?"

"Would you steal a cursed book?"

"Of course not. But I'm going to be a knight. I wouldn't steal." He took up another sapling and started whittling a point on the end.

"What's with all the weapons?" Judith asked. "And tell the truth this time, Parz—I mean, Lord Parzifal!" She added the honorific after a sidelong glance at me.

"Just east of here . . . about a mile . . . there's a dragon's hold."

"A dragon?" Judith shrieked.

"A small dragon!" Parz said, making a calming gesture I'd seen him use on his horse.

"A *small* dragon?" Judith shouted.

"It will be fine!" Parz said. "I learned about it back in King's Winter. It's a young beast we can take with just swords and these makeshift spears. It'll be good practice."

I had thought Judith's shrieking and shouting were because she was angry, but now she clapped her hands. I stared at her. She wasn't angry. She was *thrilled*.

"Wait," I said. "We haven't done *any* of the research you were talking about. We haven't spoken with any other dragon slayers. The handbook is almost completely blank! And Parz, you've pretty much said yourself you're less than half trained in this. And Judith has barely any training at all! You'll get her killed! She doesn't want to fight your 'small' dragon."

Judith's eyes had been shining like she was about to receive a gift, but now her whole expression fell, smile into frown. "Princess Mathilda," she said formally. "That is untrue. I want to fight this dragon."

"We haven't done any of the research!" I repeated.

"Not so!" Parz said. "You read about Saint Magnus and the pitch and resin and you told us about it. That's research right there."

I folded my arms, annoyed. Parz had launched this grand plan to make the *Handbook*, but I was beginning to think that, really, he didn't want me along at all—he just wanted Judith, so he had someone to fight dragons with. The *Handbook* was just a . . . a sop, to keep me from taking Judith away from him.

I was about to say this, but Judith clutched my hand. "Please understand, Tilda. We'll be back at Alder Brook before you know it . . . and I'll be a handmaiden again. But until then—I want to be a dragon slayer. This is my one chance to try something of my own."

It would be lying to say I didn't understand her. So I gave in. "You stay far back," I said. "And don't get hurt."

"I won't," she said.

Parz looked satisfied and began his spear carving again. Just then, the wind picked up in the trees. I glanced at the branches uneasily, shivering, thinking about Frau Oda's old warning.

"Oooo," Parz said, laughing. Judith joined, though I remained silent.

"We should get some sleep," I said. "There's a dragon to fight tomorrow."

chapter 7

I WOKE TO FIND PARZ STRUGGLING INTO SOME MESH armor: a mail shirt that hung to his knees and a mail coif for his head. The rest of his body was clad in padded leather pieces, though I worried for his unprotected legs and hands.

But I worried much harder for Judith. All she had to wear was some old quilted cloth armor Parz had worn in training, and it didn't fit very well.

Judith grinned at me. "Oh, Tilda, don't worry. I've little training, but I know better than to jump into the mouth of the dragon! I'll hang back and wait to make my move."

This was less reassuring than she seemed to think, especially when I overheard their plan, which didn't seem to involve any sort of hanging back and was more a "march together into the jaws of death" sort of idea.

We packed up all our gear and loaded it onto the palfrey, then put out our campfire and started upstream alongside the Willows River. I rode with Parz—only because I refused to ride alone, and I would be too slow at walking—while Judith led the laden palfrey.

The mounts were still tired from the day before, but Parz's drooping horse began to pick up his pace. "Balmung knows a fight is coming," Parz said. "See how excited he is?" The horse's ears swiveled forward and back as though listening to us.

"Balmung . . . why is that name familiar?"

I didn't have to look; I could hear the smile in Parz's voice. "Because that was the sword Siegfried used to slay Fafnir."

I giggled. Saint Catherine, I giggled! I put it down to tiredness from sleeping on the ground, though I could not help but feel that I was most certainly not myself right now. Of course, I had left myself behind at Snail Castle. I could no longer be Mathilda, Princess of Alder Brook. I would now be Tilda, errant dragon slayer, or at least the scribe to one.

"So Balmung is accustomed to battle?"

"He's used to training with me, and he's used to

practice melees, too. Now listen: If we get separated," Parz said to me and Judith, "meet up at the next town up the Rhine. It's called Upper Folkstown."

"Why would we get separated?" I asked, alarmed.

Parz's slightly crooked grin didn't look very real. "We won't! But we're going into battle, and it's just good to have a plan."

We crested a hill and came to a crumbling tower standing in the midst of a field of browning grass.

"This is it," Parz said, and unceremoniously slid me off his horse to the ground. I caught myself awkwardly with a grunt, but he was too distracted to notice.

Judith tied the palfrey to a tree, then took a spear from Parz. She stood by his right knee as he drew his sword. Together, they advanced on the tower.

I held my breath.

They moved ever more slowly as they approached, as though waiting for something to burst from the empty doorway. Parz's confusion was visible as no dragon leaped forth—he twitched and moved in the saddle half a dozen times, looking like he was going to step down. He couldn't take the horse into the tower with him, could he? The tower was too small for that.

I wondered if I should be taking notes for the *Handbook*.

Parz stood in his stirrups, about to dismount, when

a sound like an eagle's shriek combined with a bear's roar filled the air. The palfrey tied next to me tossed its head, eyes rolling back, ears swiveling anxiously. I backed away from it, afraid of its hooves.

Balmung remained calm in comparison, merely freezing in his tracks. The horse didn't move a hair even when a creature the size of a large dog launched itself out of a hole in the roof of the tower and soared overhead.

"Get down here and fight me, dragon!" Parz shouted, waving his sword.

I squinted into the bright autumn sky. A real dragon! Green-and-brown-patterned scales, a long snaky neck, thick claws, narrow wings—yes, it was a dragon, all right. I'd never seen one in person before. I liked to think that was due to some level of wisdom on the part of my family—Cousin Ivo excepted.

The dragon circled once, twice, then bent its neck like a goose before giving off another honking, roaring scream and landing right in front of Judith and Parz. The dragon was small next to Balmung, but even a large, friendly hunting hound can be imposing. And this dragon wasn't friendly.

Parz screamed something wordless at the dragon as it advanced on them. Judith scrambled backward, staying out of reach of the dragon's mouth. Another roaring scream emerged from the dragon, and the palfrey beside me lost all control, thrashing against the knots that tied it to the tree. I moved farther away, worried it might trample me, torn between putting distance between me and the palfrey and watching the fight.

Parz fumbled in a pouch at his belt as Balmung shied from the dragon. Judith threw a spear, but the dragon ducked. The dragon opened its mouth and launched forward. Parz managed to free a lump of pitch and resin from his pouch and tossed the lump into the dragon's open mouth. The dragon swallowed!

Now Judith and Parz went into full retreat, getting distance while waiting for the dragon to ignite the pitch with its inner fire.

But nothing happened. I realized: The dragon hadn't used any flame in this battle.

The dragon, slow and ungainly on the ground, took wing again, trumpeting its roar. The thrashing palfrey jerked its head desperately and succeeded in freeing itself from the tree. Before I could even try to catch the reins or say "Whoa!" the horse was gone.

With all of our belongings.

I hollered for it to come back. Neither Parz nor Judith seemed to notice me or the palfrey, intent as they were on the circling dragon above. Parz shook his sword skyward.

The dragon screeched again—and dived toward Balmung.

Balmung bolted; the last clear image I saw of Parz was the flash of pink from his open, shouting mouth in his pale face as he was carried off by his panicking horse.

Just when I thought that it might be over for Parz, the dragon slowed and turned.

"Judith!" I screamed. She was already running toward me. She didn't see the dragon behind her.

But the dragon wasn't going for Judith—the dragon was going for the palfrey, who had, in its terror, run around the edge of the clearing and now foolishly ran right at the dragon.

The dragon went in for the palfrey, landing on its back. Claws sank into saddle and bags, and the horse screamed. I screamed too.

Judith ran at me, flailing her arms. "Run!"

I turned, crutch under my arm, and made for the cover of the trees.

When Judith caught up with me, she looped her shoulder beneath mine, and we sped through the underbrush, going deeper and deeper into the forest.

"We should find Parz," I tried to tell Judith.

"Are there birds in your head? Keep going."

"I'm slowing you down—you could go back and find Parz without me!"

"*All kinds of birds,*" Judith said through clenched teeth. "Look, leaving you alone is out of the question, but even if it weren't, there's no way on earth I'm going anywhere near that dragon. Which is out of sight now. . . ." She slowed us to a walk.

I frowned. Judith was scared of the dragon, but she wasn't scared enough to leave Parz behind. But she *was* too scared to leave *me* behind, I realized. I was about to order her to go back to find Parz, then the pain in my foot and leg took away my breath.

My foot should theoretically have been thankful for the slower pace. But even the momentary respite triggered pain where, before, panic had erased it, and now it felt like I walked on daggers.

Judith was there immediately, trying to help me straighten, asking me where it hurt. I shook my head. Standing upright, I bit my knuckle and forced myself to take a step, then another, and another.

Once I got back up to a speedy walk, the keening pain flattened out into constant misery. It was better as long as I was moving.

"Do you see Parz behind us?" I asked after a moment. My voice was hoarse and raw from the earlier screaming and the current pain.

"He's nowhere to be seen. But don't worry—Balmung will keep him safe. That horse was running flat out. He'll be fine. We just have to do what he says, and meet up with him at the next town."

"What if the dragon—"

"He *said* he'll catch up to us in the next town."

I just nodded. Judith bit her lip. We kept on.

chapter 8

I WAS LIMPING FAR WORSE THAN NORMAL BY THE TIME we found a road, but I knew that if I stopped walking, it'd be nearly impossible to start again. I'd overtaxed my foot, and I was going to pay for it later.

Judith scanned the skies between tree branches as we walked. Eventually, she said, "I don't think it's flying after us."

"I hope Parz and Balmung are all right."

"I wonder how the palfrey is. Poor Felix."

"That was his name?" I asked, and somehow, knowing his name was just *awful*. I blinked back tears. "That evil, evil dragon."

Judith sniffled. "I hope Felix didn't suffer."

"I hope not, too," I said. "But either way, Felix

is gone. Along with all of our belongings." With our clothes, I realized, but more importantly, my writing box, the blank *Handbook*, and—

My stomach grumbled.

—and whatever food and coin we'd had among the three of us.

"Why didn't the pitch and resin ignite?" Judith moaned.

"The dragon didn't use any flame for the whole battle," I said. "Isn't that odd?"

Judith was quiet for a moment. "Odd," she said, her voice breaking a little on the word. "Why wouldn't it have fire? It was such a strange little dragon—it wasn't very good at flying—it didn't seem quite . . . Oh, Tilda." Judith's eyes welled with sudden tears. "I think we tried to kill a baby dragon."

"Oh no," I said, less out of sympathy for the dragon than for Judith. Judith had to help every baby everywhere, no matter what the circumstance. Human babies. Horse babies. Frog babies. That was how we had ended up with goats tromping on our heads in the middle of the night, once.

"Oh, Tilda," Judith said again, and started to cry in earnest.

"That dragon might have been too young to have fire," I said, "but it was clearly old enough to eat horses. And maybe people."

"That's not its fault! That's just its *nature*," Judith said. "Like how baby goats need to climb. No one teaches them that. They don't do it because they're good or evil. They just climb."

I squinted, thinking on the nature of the dragons in the stories of the saints. Saints had no trouble knowing dragons were evil.

I kept looking behind us, hoping we'd spy Parz's grinning face, but we didn't. But we could not in earnestness consider going back. My foot could not have withstood it.

When we reached the wide Rhine, we turned upriver, hopefully toward Upper Folkstown.

"We should find a place to eat and rest," Judith said.

"With what money?"

"I could sell my hair," Judith said.

I considered, hands tapping the dullish eating knife at my belt. Hers wasn't very long, not reaching even to the middle of her back. She'd had a fever a few years ago, and it had been cut off then.

"We'll sell mine. More money."

Judith's eyes went wide. "Your mother will be *so* angry if you do that. I can't let you."

"Why will she be angry?" I asked.

"Well, she deplores women wearing false hair, for one thing—"

"That's because she deplores the fact that it's cut off of dead people, I think."

"Yes, but. What are you going to do when you get back to Alder Brook with short hair? You'll have to buy some dead-people hair, then. And thus Princess Isobel will be angry."

"I would think she'd rather we didn't starve, in the long run," I said. Which would be true. My mother was a pragmatist in many ways. Judith wasn't wrong, though. My mother would also be angry, and the option of not wearing my hair in long braids wouldn't *be* an option, because that was not what princesses did.

I almost said, "Good thing I'm not going back to Alder Brook, then." But I bit my tongue and handed Judith the knife.

"Are you *sure?*"

"Just go gently," I said.

The knife was so dull, it took forever to saw through my thick braids, and each section of hair seemed to pull exceptionally hard before it was severed. I wished for my sharp little penknife, but that was yet another thing we'd lost with Felix the palfrey.

My head felt naked afterward, but I felt free, freer than I had when I'd turned my back on Alder Brook. I hefted the braids in my hands with some amazement. They reached the ground. "No wonder my scalp aches sometimes."

Judith nodded, and we went into the town, which was a pretty jumble of newish wattle-and-daub houses dotted with older stone buildings.

The town was almost entirely empty, which was to be expected with all the ripe vineyards around. We could see distant dots moving among the terraced vines. It seemed like *everyone* was recruited for the harvest. We couldn't even find an alehouse that was open.

We knocked at the kitchen doors of all the largest houses and eventually found someone who wanted to buy my braids. We took part of our payment in dark bread, sausages, cheese, apples, and small ale.

The mistress of the house who bought our hair dispatched a maidservant to finish dealing with us. The maidservant said, "You're awful young to be here in Upper Folkstown during the grape harvest."

"Seems like a very late harvest," I said, not certain what she meant.

"It is," the maidservant said with some pride. "But our valley is famous for our late harvest of grapes, which makes the most special, sweetest wine. Or—we were. Now get along. You'd best be to the next town before curfew."

"Thanks, but we were looking to stay here—"

"No." The maid's eyes were round and blue and a little blank. "You don't want to be anywhere *near* here tonight. Move along quick as you can. Before sunset. It's First Night."

"What's First Night?"

The maid looked out over our heads at the vineyards that threaded the mountainsides. "The end of the world."

She shut the door.

Judith and I stared at each other, then turned to leave.

Immediately, I fell—my foot wobbled right, my knee wobbled left, and I crashed right down off the doorstep of the house, landing on my shoulder and jarring it. The breath left me in a whoosh.

My leg and foot had seized up completely, angry with the overwork of the day.

"We'll get a room at a guesthouse," Judith said.

"Absolutely not. We can't afford it, if we want to keep eating!"

"You need some proper care. We'll *find* a guesthouse."

I acquiesced, but there was no guesthouse that would have us. The first and third guesthouses in the town were empty and barred, and the second one refused to rent to us. "If it weren't First Night . . . ," the landlady said. "But it is. Now get on away from here, as far as you can, before you regret it."

"Well, what are we going to do?" Judith said,

lowering me to the doorstep of the last guesthouse and giving my leg a vigorous rubbing.

"Parz is planning to look for us here," I said. "We'll need to leave him a message that we've moved on . . . or just go camp out of sight of all these mad people, and come back in the morning."

"Both," Judith said. We left a message with the town watch, and they, too, told us to move on before nightfall.

We weren't much beyond the shadow of the town wall before I knew I couldn't hobble any farther.

"We have to turn back," Judith said.

"I can't make it back," I said, tears leaking from the corners of my eyes. Involuntary tears—I wasn't crying or anything.

Judith scanned the landscape. On our right ran the mighty Rhine; on the left, a terraced vineyard rose above us. There were no harvesters here—they'd all been working closer to town.

Two terraces up squatted a small barn, though that might have been too grand a term for the building.

"I can get you there," Judith said grimly, and she half carried, half dragged me up the mountain and deposited me inside the structure. It was a storage hut, full of trellis pieces and bits for repair, tools for harvesting, baskets, and buckets. There was no convenient pile of hay, as there should be in a proper barn, but at least it would be some shelter from the night frost.

Judith opened the barn door wide and built a small fire at the door's mouth, so we could have some heat and yet vent the smoke.

The flesh of my foot was hot, red and tight, once we had my shoe and stocking off to examine it. I had incipient blisters nearly everywhere.

"It's going to be a long day," I said, even though it was already somewhat past noon.

"I'm going to fetch a healer."

"What would we pay a healer with?" I asked, and Judith didn't mention leaving again. "I just need to rest it."

We knew that was true. This had happened before. There really wasn't much to do for my foot but to apply heat and cold and bandage those blisters. To that end, Judith put some stones in the fire and left some in the shadows outside, and we tried using them. But the cold wasn't very cold, so Judith jogged down to the Rhine and brought cool, wet stones back up.

It wasn't quite the same as Frau Oda's hot and cold poultices reeking of mustard seed, but it would do.

We ate sausages while watching the round moon race to rise before the sun set, and tied more wet stones from the Rhine to my foot. Judith said, handing me an apple, "What do you think the maid meant,

'It's the end of the world'?"

I shrugged, turning the apple over in my hands but not biting into it. I wasn't hungry after all the sausage. "A generation ago, everyone thought the world would end because it had been a thousand years since Christ's birth. Father Ripertus said that in some places they never quite got over that, and every few years prepare for the end all over again. Maybe this is one of those places. Anyway, it doesn't matter—we're out of the town."

"And there's no one else around," Judith said.

That was worrisome. But I couldn't say exactly why. We made uncomfortable beds from our cloaks on the dirt floor and fell asleep, the moon shining bright on our faces through the barn door.

THUNDER WOKE ME.

"Strange," Judith murmured. "I thought it was clear tonight."

"It is," I said, staring out the barn door at the sky full of stars.

The thunder roared louder.

And then the shaking began.

At first, I almost didn't notice it. It was like being rocked in a cradle in the beginning, but then the shaking got harder and harder. The beams of the barn creaked and moaned. Judith and I got to our feet, no longer even a little drowsy.

We would have run outside right then, for fear the barn would come down on our heads, but outside was no better. The vines were tossing on their trellises, and leaves scuttled past in long chains.

"Storm and earthquake," Judith cried. "It really is the end of the world!"

Then came the light. It was so bright, I flung my cloak over Judith and me, pulling us down to the ground with the fabric over our heads. Even through the cloak, the light turned the inside of my eyelids bright red. The noise of the wind and the shaking rose to a steady, low hum, like giant bees in a field of flowers.

Then the noise died away. The light dimmed.

My skin felt pricked by pins and needles. I threw back the cloak. Judith and I stared at each other: The barn was bright, far brighter than it had been in moonlight and firelight, though still dimmer than in the sun, or in the blinding light that had preceded this.

And the silence was vast and strange. So quiet, it almost burned the ears. There should have been something to hear, and my ears strained to listen for a sound, any sound. Judith got to her feet, but her footsteps made almost no noise—flat, muted thuds that I could barely hear.

Judith hit the side of her head, as if tapping water from her ears.

I hummed, testing my voice. It felt flat and lost in this silence. "Are you all right?" I asked.

"Ahhhhh," Judith sang with two fingers pressed to her throat. She nodded, and helped me to my feet.

From outside came a noise like distant war drums.

chapter 9

JUDITH WAS FIRST OUT THE BARN DOOR. I FOLLOWED on her heels but could not keep pace.

Outside, in the windless calm, a strange light lay over everything. It was like the light that comes in a late-afternoon thunderstorm, when the sunrays stab golden across the sky from the west, vividly lighting up banks of onrushing coal-colored clouds. The whole world seems lit by witch light during those storms.

In the terraced vineyards near Upper Folkstown, I saw the same kind of light—only with no sun. The world was bright but the sky was dark, the stars and moon now blotted by clouds. The light came from nowhere, from no single source. It was true witch light.

Two terraces above the barn, a great, gleaming creature ran, trampling vines flat with its gigantic hooves.

The creature was a horse. A huge, golden horse, wearing a golden saddle, an iron bridle, and two bulging saddlebags.

I tried to speak, but in the airless calm, my voice died in my throat.

A shriek—a battle cry, like nothing I'd ever heard before—rose, entirely bone-chilling; the cry was followed by the jolting crack of hooves hitting the earth and splitting it open. Another enormous horse, this one copper, bore down on Judith. It reared in front of her and struck out with its front hooves, hitting Judith in the shoulder. She went down with a muffled cry. I choked on my breath, unsure of what to do.

The copper horse stared coldly down at Judith, a malevolent intelligence in its eyes. *It's going to trample her to death.*

I screamed some wordless denial at it and ran forward, waving my arms, to plant myself between Judith and the horse.

The copper horse reared—and I don't exactly know what happened next, because I thought for sure it was about to trample *both* of us, but a blur of silver caught the corner of my eye—and then an impact against my ribs pushed me aside. It was gentle, not painful, and it seemed that for one moment, I was floating above the earth, before I found myself standing six paces farther north than I had been.

Between Judith and the copper horse—between *me* and the copper horse—stood a silver mare. She faced the copper horse with flared nostrils and flattened ears, baring teeth.

The copper horse backed away.

I made a noise then. It might have been a squeak of fear. It might have been the words I had lost in my screaming, trying and failing to find form on my lips. The point is, I made a noise and I shouldn't have, because in no way did I want to draw the attention of any of the horses—gold, copper, or silver.

The silver horse wheeled around and stared me down, bathing my face with her hot breath.

I stared back, frozen in terror. All I could see was the sharp, hard feet that could grind me into dust, the giant teeth that could rend my flesh from the bones. They might not be a dragon's tearing teeth, but they were no less fearsome.

Not too far away, the copper horse started trampling the vines—a fast but deliberate movement, as it methodically tore down and pulverized the whole row of grapes. Puzzled, I glanced over, then back. Judith's auburn hair caught my eye.

"Judith?" I whispered.

The silver horse showed her teeth again, and I flinched.

"I'm all right," Judith whimpered. "I mean, other than my shoulder."

The silver horse did not look around at Judith's voice, but when the copper horse drew near again, the mare sent it away with an angry snort.

The silver mare bent her head toward me and showed her teeth again. *She's going to take my nose off,* I thought, shaking, and turned my cheek aside. I took a half step back, then waited, unsure of how close the golden horse was, and unwilling to take my eyes off the silver mare. She had saved us from the copper horse, but her lips curled from her teeth again and again and again. I cowered away from her, praying she wouldn't bite me.

"Tilda!" Judith called in a low voice. "She—she's not threatening you. She's fighting that bit in her mouth."

I glanced up at the horse, my tremors subsiding as my curiosity increased. I studied the horse. She was silver, from teeth to tail, and this was certainly amazing; but amazing as well were the elaborate, bejeweled saddle and fittings of silver she wore. Bulging saddlebags of cloth of silver rested both ahead of the pommel and behind the cantle.

But her bridle was a different story; it was not

silver but dark iron, wrapped around the mare's face like a cage—and it didn't belong.

Judith was right.

I reached up to touch the bridle. The mare quieted, no longer making her teeth-baring face.

"How do I take the bridle off?" I called back softly. Our voices still sounded strange and flat in the dead-calm air.

"Reach up—grab that topmost piece of the bridle, between the ears, and just pull forward and down."

My hands fumbled to obey Judith's instructions. My fingers skimmed up to the topmost piece between the ears, hooked around it, and pulled it forward.

Immediately, the bit dropped out of the horse's mouth, and the whole iron bridle fell to the ground.

The silver mare shook herself and grunted.

Behind me, I heard the continued trampling of the golden horse. Beyond the silver mare, the copper horse edged closer to me again. The silver horse wheeled about and stared down the copper horse.

I was uncomfortable with the silver horse's massive rear hooves so easily in striking distance of me, but I wasn't scared witless anymore. I sidled over to Judith, then crouched next to her.

"What's wrong with your shoulder?" I whispered.

"It's . . . It might be broken."

"Thunder weather!" I swore. We couldn't just slap

a hot rock on a broken bone. Of course, we couldn't even do *that* surrounded by these horses.

"Do you think you can get up?"

"We'll see."

We managed to get Judith to her feet. The copper horse—another mare—flattened her ears, but the silver horse blocked her approach.

"Let's get you to the barn," I said, and together we moved slowly across the terrace to the little wooden building. The silver mare kept pace, always placing herself between us and the copper horse.

"I've never seen anything like them," Judith said once we were inside the barn. I stood in the doorway, studying them. All three gleamed like metal; all three wore bejeweled tack and bulging saddlebags. The golden and copper horses each had dark iron bridles as well.

Three horses made of the three royal metals, here in Upper Folkstown.

The copper horse tried to approach the barn, but the silver mare headed her off again.

I watched the copper horse closely. She was making the same lip-curling face that the silver mare had. She flicked an ear, watching me watch her.

I stepped out of the barn.

The silver horse stepped forward, as if to push me back inside; but while I was still wary of her, I was no longer exactly scared. I was the mouse who had removed the thorn from the lion's paw. I put my hand out to brush the silver horse's neck, to show her I would not be herded back into the barn.

"I'm, um, fine. You can . . . well, you can stand guard, but stop interfering."

Slowly, cautiously, I edged toward the copper horse. Her aggression had died away, and she simply stood there, waiting for me, while she fought her bit.

When I reached the copper mare, I waited a moment for her to quiet, then pulled off her bridle, too. This time I caught it, not letting it fall to the ground.

The copper horse dropped her nose to my head and snorted.

"Don't chew my hair off," I whispered.

She blew into my ear and then sort of grunted at me. Not a whinny—something else.

I backed away from the copper horse, the bridle looped around my wrist, and looked up at the golden stallion still trampling the vineyard to dust. He was many terraces above us now—he had destroyed nearly the whole vineyard. I wondered if he wanted to be free of his bridle, too, but there was a wildness to him that made me too afraid to go and try.

"I don't know that my foot could handle it, anyway," I said regretfully.

A light wind ruffled my hair. The strange silence disappeared beneath a crack of new thunder, and clouds roiled above us.

The horses started to mill about, staring up at the sky and the fading witch light.

"What's going on?" Judith called from the doorway of the barn.

"I don't know!"

A low and piercing note filled the air, making the hair on my arms stand up and a weird shudder run down my back. The note came again, and then again. The horses kept staring into the sky. The golden horse galloped down the hill toward us. "Is that a hunting horn?" I shrieked over the noise.

Lightning flickered above us, illuminating the clouds. And among the clouds were the shapes of horses and hounds.

"The Wild Hunt!" Judith screamed, hanging on to the doorframe of the barn with her good arm. "Tilda, get in here!"

I started for the barn, still carrying the iron bridle, but there was no time. The Wild Hunt touched down in the vineyard.

chapter 10

I STRUGGLED TO REACH THE BARN EVEN AS THE LEAD hounds of the Wild Hunt flowed around me and past. Their heads came to my shoulder. They were utterly silent, not baying like hounds usually do, and they kept their distance. I wasn't even brushed by a wagging tail as they raced by. They ignored me utterly.

Unfortunately, the same could not be said for the huntsmen.

The lead horse was darkest gray and yet brightly shining, and so enormous that it dwarfed the metal horses. And it was ridden by a helmeted horseman who seemed to have no face or eyes beneath his helm, just a burning, red maw.

No—not horseman. Horsewoman. There was a

distinctly female shape to the Hunt leader's body.

The Hunter reined in her shining horse and stared down at me.

"Ride with us," said a voice like a whisper, but so loud I wanted to huddle down and clamp my hands over my ears.

"No," I said. "I don't ride. I can't. I was never taught."

And then I realized I had refused the Wild Hunt.

You are never supposed to refuse the Wild Hunt. At best, you agree to go with them, and maybe after they are done with you, you retain your sanity, and possibly they reward you—or just as likely, you go mad and get no reward.

But at least if you accommodate them, you have a chance. Refuse them, and—

"Then you will be punished," said the Hunter.

I stood as straight as I could, shoulders back, still holding the iron bridle loosely in one hand. "It's not my fault," I shouted. "You shouldn't punish me because I don't know how to ride!" I just wanted to register my objection. I didn't think that would stop her. Which is good, because it didn't.

The Hunter raised her sword, and I closed my eyes. I really hadn't expected to die like this, and so young. . . .

The blow never fell. Instead, a whoosh of air

ruffled my hair, and thunderous hoofbeats shook the ground.

The silver mare had put herself between me and the Hunter's sword. The mare reared up and struck the blade with her hooves, raising sparks that seemed to fly a league.

The red pit where the Hunter's face should have been flamed like coals under a breeze. "You dare!" Her voice at full shout sounded less like a single voice and more like the screams of a thousand crows.

It was the stupidest thing I'd ever thought to do—I could so easily have been struck by the mare who was trying to defend me, as well as by the Hunter—but I put my hand to the silver mare's neck and tried to place myself between her and the Hunter.

"Leave her alone!" I bellowed, shaking the iron bridle in the face of the Hunter's horse.

Well, I tried to bellow. My voice was more like that of a mouse than an ox.

The great, shining gray horse of the Hunter shied from the iron bridle much to my shock.

The Hunter regained control of her stallion and looked down at me. Her voice was pure menace. "You have failed, Mathilda of Alder Brook." I cringed to hear my full name spoken in that crow-screaming voice. "You have freed two of the three, but the Aurum still belongs to me."

"What? What are you talking about? The horses? I wasn't even—I didn't even *try* to do anything! How can I fail at something I didn't even *try*?"

"Ignorance does not make the wrong choice into the right one. And fate is sealed by choices," she said.

In the distance, a rooster crowed. All the dogs and horses of the Hunt pricked their ears.

"Dawn is your savior." The Hunter's yawning red maw seemed to blaze. "We will meet again, Mathilda. And then you *will* repay the debt you owe me."

She gestured to one of the other hunters, who put a horn to his lips and blew.

The call of the horn rose and swelled, seeming to reverberate in my very bones, making my teeth ache. I knew if it continued, it was going to shatter my skull—but it didn't keep going.

The great hounds slid away like quicksilver. The horses and their riders jogged up the mountainside, flattening the few surviving rows of vines. The golden horse with the iron bridle ran with them as they charged straight up—but instead of cresting the peak, they rode on up, into the clouds and the storm, which retreated across the sky.

The silver horse and the copper one remained, gleaming in the fading witch light, and watched the Wild Hunt depart.

Dawn broke over the hills, driving apart the last

clouds that had accompanied the Hunt.

The silver horse faced me with a sigh, and then snuffled my hair. The copper horse retreated slightly and watched us warily.

"What just happened?" Judith asked somberly, coming out of the barn. "Did you— Tilda! You refused the Wild Hunt and lived to tell about it!"

"Yes, but—uh—but—" It was hard to talk with a horse's nose buried in my hair, her breath all warm and whuffling, her long whiskers tickling my ears. "But now I owe a debt?" I couldn't keep the panic out of my voice.

"You stole their horses!"

"I did not steal them!" I tried to duck away from the horse's insistent nuzzles. "I set them . . . free."

"How much do two magical Wild Hunt horses cost, exactly?" Judith asked. "I don't suppose you can pay that off in gold marks."

"No, I suppose not." As if Alder Brook had enough reserve in its treasury to even consider that. As if I had any claim on Alder Brook's treasury anymore. "I'm afraid it's going to be one of those awful prices, like my first-born child, or my immortal soul. . . ."

Judith moved to put an arm around me for comfort, then winced, clutching her shoulder.

"Judith, I'm so sorry!" I said. "We need to get you to a bonesetter right away!"

Judith grunted agreement.

I went back to the barn to pack up our meager possessions—all food at this point—and then we started down the road toward Upper Folkstown.

Judith couldn't assist me any more than I could assist her, between her shoulder and my crutch. My foot was tender and unpleasant to walk on, but I was in many respects in better shape than Judith. For one thing, I was used to my pain, and she was far from accustomed to hers. She could walk all right, but every step was jarring.

The metal horses came too. The silver mare kept pace beside me. And she didn't shake me off or back away when I occasionally reached out to her for balance.

WE REACHED THE TOWN gates and knocked for admission at the night portal. It was dawn, but towns did not open their gates until the sun was well up.

"Who goes there?" asked the watchman.

"This is P— Lady Agilwarda . . . of Oak Hill," Judith said, pointing at me. "I am her servant."

Judith was a terrible liar.

The night watchman looked at me. "Milady. You're fair young to be out on your own."

"I have my servant," I said serenely.

"What are *those*?" he asked, craning his neck toward the mares.

"Uh . . . horses?"

"Strange horses," the watchman said. "That one looks"—he paused, then clearly decided *silver* was a ridiculous thought—"white. What were you doing out on First Night?"

"First Night?"

"Three nights in a row, round Saint Martin's Eve, our town gets shook by thunder and storm, and when we wake up, a third of our grape harvest is gone, until by the last night, our whole harvest is gone."

Judith and I looked at each other. "Yes, well," I said. "It might be *these* horses from the Wild Hunt trampling your vineyards."

The watchman gaped.

"Lady Agilwarda stopped them," Judith said. "Lady Agilwarda . . . seems to have tamed them."

"Liar!" I whispered, and elbowed her in the side. Then immediately regretted it when she winced.

"Horses?" the watchman asked. "From the Wild Hunt? The mayor is going to want to hear about this."

"We need a bonesetter first," I said.

"Come inside, come inside. I'll take you to the mayor's house, then get you a bonesetter," he said, and cracked open not the night portal, which was barely wide enough for a large man to clamber through, but the gate of the town itself.

We entered the town, and true to his word, the

watchman led us up to the mayor's house. It took no effort to roust the mayor, for he, like everyone left in town, had been sitting vigil through the night. Before I quite knew it, the watchman was ringing a bell and several score of the town's citizens gathered around, holding torches and lanterns. They stared at us while we tried to explain what had happened. They stared even harder at the horses. How could they not? The mares were bigger than any warhorse I'd seen by at least several hands. And they shone like the moon and a copper dinner plate.

There were rumblings among the people as the mayor thanked us—calling me Lady Agilwarda—extensively for saving most of the harvest, and handed us a disappointingly deflated bag that ostensibly held a cash reward.

Someone in the crowd began a chant. At first I didn't understand they were cheering for me, but they were smiling, clapping their hands and stomping their feet as they chanted the words: *Wein Fürstin. Wein Fürstin.*

Wine Princess.

chapter 11

AFTER THE CROWD TOASTED US WITH BLACKBERRY cordial for a bit (since there was no wine to be had in the town), we were invited to the local guest-house to sleep until the Martinmas feast began at midday.

The horses trailed along during all of this. They were calm in the crowds, as long as no one tried to touch them, and no one *did* try to touch them—twice.

They followed us to the guesthouse, as well, and we stood in the innyard for a long moment, staring at the horses while they stared at us.

"We're, um, going inside," Judith said.

"Looks like the bonesetter is here," I said, sighting the watchman coming toward us, accompanied by an awkward young man. "You go ahead. I'll . . . see . . . to the . . . horses."

"I can help with that," a familiar voice said.

"Parz!" I whirled about, heart soaring. I threw my arms around his neck and received a swift, tight hug in return. He was alive! I stepped back, embarrassed by my display, but he kindly made no remark. "What happened to you?"

"What happened to *you*?" he asked, eyes wide at Judith.

So we told him, while the bonesetter determined that Judith hadn't actually broken anything, she had just managed to yank her shoulder out of its joint. The resetting of the joint looked worse than the actual knocking out, but she said it felt better almost immediately.

We *told* Parz everything that had happened to us, but *explaining* it was a different matter entirely.

Parz's story was simpler but had more tragedy.

"Balmung bucked me off and ran away," Parz said, his jaw clenching and unclenching. "I followed his trail as best I could but . . ." He shook his head. "He wasn't wounded, so he's got a good chance. Horses like to go home when they're scared. . . . Wouldn't be surprised if he shows up at Boar House in a day or two."

He didn't quite look like he believed it, and he

stared sadly at the ground.

"I'm sorry," I said, putting my hand on his arm in a gesture of condolence. Almost absently, he clutched my fingers and held on.

"What about Felix?" Judith asked from where the bonesetter was fashioning her a sling. "He looked—"

"I don't know. The dragon managed to pull some of our baggage off him in the first two strikes, and I didn't find many bloodstains when I went back. . . . But Felix was long gone when I returned, wherever he went."

"So . . . none of our possessions were there?" Judith asked, looking pointedly at the saddlebag he had slung over one shoulder.

"A few."

A surge of hope rose in me at that moment, but I tried to quell it. I didn't want to be disappointed if all Parz had managed to salvage was a dress or a pair of stockings. "Everything was scattered to the four winds. But I did find—" Parz plunged his hand into the saddlebag and pulled out something I'd not dared to hope for: the blank *Handbook*. He offered it to me.

I grabbed the book and held it to my chest in a strange little hug. "Thank you, Parz," I said. "I don't suppose you found my writing box?"

Parz's half smile fell. "No, I'm sorry."

I tried not to lose all cheer at that. The book really

wasn't much use without a pen, but there were all sorts of birds out there willing to donate a quill or two. Just . . . There was no replacing the metal stylus for scribing wax tablets, which conformed perfectly to my hand. Nor the ink I'd mixed myself to the exact consistency I loved. Nor the little wooden box of pins to mark the spacing on a blank page, which Father Ripertus had carved for me. Nor the perfectly sharpened penknife with the mother-of-pearl handle that my father had given me before he left Alder Brook. And the box itself? It wasn't anything fancy, but it was stained from the ink of all my years of writing and copying, a sign of all my hard work.

I turned away so neither Parz nor Judith could see the bitter tear that slipped down my cheek. I closed my eyes.

Something huge and warm and wet touched my forehead. I opened my eyes into the face of the silver mare, who finished her long lick with a good swipe across my hair.

"Er, thank you?"

She nickered.

"We should water them," Parz said.

"Almost done here," Judith said, and waved us on.

Parz went into the stable to get buckets, and I followed to help him.

The horses in turn trailed after us. Parz froze and

looked behind us. "This is a little strange," he whispered. "Try going into that foaling stall, there. . . . See if they follow you."

I went into the wide box stall, which had an opening to an outdoor pen, and the horses came in with me. I sidled out of the stall, praying I wouldn't get squished. They didn't try to follow me back out.

"Is this it?" I asked. "Are they going to stay in the stable?"

"Maybe," Parz said. He gave them hay, which they ignored, and water, which they played with.

"Should we remove their tack?" I asked.

Parz didn't look away from them. "Sure. Go ahead."

"Are you—are you scared of them, Parz?"

"A little!"

"Well, I'm scared, too!" I said.

He took a deep breath, and said, "All right." He walked into the stall and approached the silver horse, showing absolutely no fear. He unloaded the horse's saddlebags and slung them into the aisle. They thunked and clinked when they landed. Then he removed the horse's silver saddle, which he treated a little more gently.

"Amazing," he muttered, carrying the saddle past me.

"Is it heavy as silver?" I asked.

"Not even, yet it feels like silver to the touch. And just look at these amethysts and sapphires! Those have to be real. Look at how they shine." He glanced around and then bent over to bite at the edge of the saddle, like one would bite a coin to make sure it was the proper metal. "Ow," Parz exhaled. He examined the spot where he'd bitten down. "It's silver all the way through."

I stifled a laugh, then faced the stall door. I squared my shoulders and lifted my chin. "All right, tell me what to do," I said. If Parz could swallow his fear, so could I.

As Parz called out directions, I started divesting the copper mare of her tack and baggage. Her tack's gemstones were all rubies and aquamarines, and the heavy saddlebags made interesting noises when I put them down.

The saddle almost overbalanced me completely, but Parz took it from me as soon as I was free of the stall. "Do you want to bite this one, too?"

"No, thank you," Parz said.

Once both horses were free of their gear, they shook themselves joyfully and danced around a little bit.

"Let's brush them down," I said, grabbing up a comb and marching into the stall with the silver mare.

She nickered softly and nuzzled my cheek.

"Hey there," I said.

I lifted the comb to her beautiful silver hair, and suddenly Parz was next to me, showing me how to curry her with circular motions from neck to hindquarters, and then how to flick away the dirt I'd raised. "If you don't throw up a plume of dust, you're not doing it right," he said. "Instead, you're driving the dirt you curried up back under the hair."

"Brushing a horse is more complicated than I thought."

He nodded. "It is. But horses are easy compared to hawks."

"Do you have a hawk?"

"No. Not currently. My father was falconer to Lord Frederick One-Eye, though, before he married my mother and became lord of Hare Hedge."

Ah. Parz's mother was an heiress, same as me, though Hare Hedge was a minor holding compared to Alder Brook. What did that make Parz? It would be rude to ask outright, which was why I never had. But he couldn't be his mother's heir if he'd been sent off to squire for a knight as old and as powerless as Sir Kunibert. A younger son, then, of a minor lord.

We worked in silence for a time, until I began to notice some subtle color variations in the horse's coat. She had a few black hairs in among the silver, but when we brushed them, the black seemed to slough away and reveal more silver hair beneath. And there was depth of color to the silver, with faint tones of orange, blue, violet. You saw that, sometimes, in silver that had been handled a lot.

"Like old coins," Parz murmured. "Or old jewelry." He picked at three long tail hairs that had adhered to his clothing and held them up to the light.

"Exactly what I was thinking." I sighed. "She's beautiful."

"Indeed she is," Parz said, and started pointing out her impressive features: a long, lean neck with a slight arch; well-proportioned limbs; a wide, deep chest. I had no idea why these things mattered, but I listened anyway.

After we were done brushing down the horses, I offered the silver mare a grain bucket. She put her nose politely inside, lapped out a few grains, chewed them thoughtfully—and spit them out at my feet.

"You're . . . not hungry, I guess?" I asked.

She blew warm, horsey breath into my face, and stamped a foot.

"I don't think they like grain," I said.

Parz frowned. "They'll eat when they're hungry," he said doubtfully.

"There you are!" Judith said from the end of the stable. She came forward into our pools of lamplight, her right arm folded up in a sling.

"Judith! Feeling better?"

"Ugh," Judith said. "I'm tender, but yes, feeling much better."

Once the horses were truly set, though they wanted none of the food or water we offered them, we gathered in an empty stall and flopped exhaustedly into piles of hay.

We were silent for a long moment, until Judith said, "What's in their saddlebags?"

Our heads all swiveled as if we were a family of owls to look at the bags lying in the aisle. Parz got up and dragged the two nearest saddlebags over—one copper, one silver—and threw open the first flap.

Hand to fire, the room shone brighter from the bounty inside. Heaps of precious metal seemed to be contained therein. At first I thought it was coins, but from the copper bag Parz lifted out one by one all the pieces of a full suit of mail armor: leggings, hood, shirt, collar, and mittens, and all the padding to be worn beneath it, quilted in a fabric that looked like shimmering copper silk.

From the silver bag, Parz pulled out a silver bridle first. Judith and I both said, "Ah!" at the same time, and exchanged a glance. Parz went on to remove a silver sword with scabbard and belt, and two silver daggers with sheaths, all bejeweled in amethysts and sapphires. There was a belt of silver, and a surcoat of the silky stuff in argent and purple, and a cloak to match.

We opened the other two bags and found that there were identical sets of equipment: two full suits of matching armor, two sets of weapons, and two bridles.

Parz stared at the copper-mesh armor coat in his hands. "Imagine fighting dragons with these horses."

I said, "If they wanted to fight dragons. I think that's up to them."

"There are three of us," Judith pointed out. "And two of them. Regardless."

I sighed with regret. "I'm not a fighter. Never will be."

"One horse for each of us to fight with," Parz said, toying with the long tail hairs he'd collected earlier. "If they want," he added hastily.

Judith set her mouth. "The silver mare belongs to Tilda. *Both* horses belong to Tilda."

"I don't think these horses *belong* to anyone," I said.

"That's true," Parz said. "But I've been watching the silver mare. She is deeply curious about the world. She likes smaller creatures—she was fascinated by the innkeeper's dog—but she does, in her horsey way, just *love* you, Tilda."

I must have looked dubious, because he said, "You told me the story yourself. I think the silver one is the lead mare. And she knows you for a lead mare, too."

"I beg your pardon?"

"You leaped to protect me from the horses," Judith said. "You leaped to protect the horses from the Hunter. You're the lead mare."

"I—I—" I fell silent. We *all* fell silent, for a long moment, I think each of us considering what life with these horses might be like. Parz started weaving the tail hairs into a little braid.

"What are you going to do with all of this *stuff*, Tilda?" Judith asked.

"*I* am not going to do anything with it. It belongs to them. And they belong to themselves, maybe, or to the Wild Hunt. I wouldn't steal from either."

"Me neither," Judith said adamantly, and yawned again.

I laughed a little, not glancing at Parz. I could see he was restless and itchy, and wanted to decide which horse belonged to whom. But I caught Judith's yawn and realized I was so far beyond tired, I was in another country altogether.

"Let's sleep here," I said, and almost before we had agreed to it, I was asleep.

WE SLEPT UNTIL THE Martinmas festivities awakened us.

Bonfires were started, and fat geese were cooked.

People cheered when they saw us, and offered us roasted goose legs and hand pies filled with blackberries, and when the cordial ran out, we drank drafts of crushed grapes that hadn't even thought of turning to wine yet.

I must have eaten a dozen tiny rolls shaped like horse hooves. Saint Martin's feast always features goose and hoof-shaped bread, because when the cardinals came to offer him the job of pope, he ran off and hid in the stables with the horses until the geese honked and gave him away.

Everywhere I went, the silver mare followed. I'd thought we had latched the stable door, but obviously that wasn't a barrier to the silver mare. Though she'd refused grain, she stole cordial and juice out of my cup when I wasn't looking. She wasn't always polite about the people who wanted to touch her—I think she bit more than a few fingers, and I know she kicked someone, but she was nice to the children.

The townsfolk who had left for the three nights of earthquakes and storms started to trickle back in on the rumors that the harvest problem was over, and the celebration's pitch rose. Musicians found each other, and dancing began. The local lord came down from his high castle in the evening, accompanied by a few of his vassals, and there were speeches. A handsome knight put a wreath of bright autumn leaves and ripe grain on my head like a crown; the children tried to put another such crown on the silver mare, but she flung it off.

Parz lost all of his money in a dice game, and Judith gained it all back for him, even with her arm in a sling. I won a singing contest against some eight-year-olds who shouldn't have goaded me into it. And we all ate and laughed. I grinned so hard, I thought my face would crack open like an eggshell and my brain would drop out like the yolk.

Maybe it was the relief of the whole town we felt; maybe it was the freedom of being on our own. I just knew I'd never been so happy.

The knight who'd given me the wreath listened carefully during the third recitation of the events with the Wild Hunt and afterward introduced himself to us as Sir Egin. He was particularly charming, kissing my hand and praising my bravery.

"Would you care to dance, milady?" Sir Egin asked. He stroked his thick blond beard and smiled down at me.

I was startled by that invitation, considering I hadn't even been trying to hide my foot or crutch or anything. It had to be fairly obvious that I wasn't capable of dancing.

"Before you say no—" he said, and lifted me into his arms and spun me around three times.

It was the fastest I'd ever moved. Ever!

"Oh!" I said, half dizzy from the movement, and stumbled a little against Sir Egin when he set me back on my feet.

The silver mare came close and thrust her head under my arm, effectively removing my hand from Sir Egin's and forcing me to step back from him. Judith spoke in my ear. "Tilda, I need you."

"Another time, Sir Egin," I said, attempting a gracious smile.

He smiled back, equally gracious—but not before a shadow darkened his eyes for a moment. He bowed deeply and turned to leave.

I frowned. Why had there been that flicker of . . . well, it wasn't annoyance, or even anger . . . when I'd refused him? What had it been?

Jealousy? Hatred?

I shivered. He had no right to be jealous. No reason to hate.

I turned to Judith, noting that she appeared to have acquired a very fine silver-and-copper chain around her neck. Where had that come from?

"Well?" I asked. "What's the matter?"

She didn't speak until Egin was well out of earshot. "The matter is that Sir Egin just buried his seventh wife," she said. "And he's probably looking for the eighth."

"I'm only thirteen!"

Judith glanced at Sir Egin's retreating back. "And do you think that matters to someone who's buried seven wives?"

chapter 12

THE CELEBRATION LASTED INTO THE NIGHT, AND WE were foolish enough to stay for the whole of it. It wasn't that we forgot about possible pursuit by Cousin Ivo; it was more that we had been through so much with the dragon and the Wild Hunt that it felt like weeks had passed instead of just a few days. But there was also Judith's shoulder to be careful of, and my foot besides.

We fell asleep in the stable, curled around goose-filled bellies in the loose straw of the stall across from the horses, while bonfires burned down to cinders outside. We were warm and cozy in the stable even though the first truly cold wind of autumn began to blow.

I woke in the middle of the night to the noise of footsteps and rustling in the metal horses' stall; a sharp blow and a withering human groan preceded running footsteps that quickly faded into the distance. Judith said, "What was that?"

"Thwarted theft, I think," Parz said with a smile in his voice. "Well, a burned child avoids the fire. They won't be back."

I fretted. "That thief might not be, but what about other thieves?"

"There might be a dozen more thieves, and I wouldn't want to be stuck in their skins for anything. Those horses are strong as bears and twice as ornery, Princess. They'll be fine."

We woke to a cloudy morning and the tolling of church bells. We felt obligated to go to mass, but as soon as that duty was done, we returned to the stables and loaded the horses up again with their tack and baggage.

"Whether or not they continue to follow us, *we* can't carry this stuff," I said.

What we couldn't quite work out, though, was where we were going. We had discussed it on the way to mass, and then again on the way back, and still hadn't agreed. Parz wanted to find another dragon slayer to talk to, but the only one he knew of besides

Sir Kunibert lived far to the south in the Alps. Judith bit her lip and said we should consider returning to Alder Brook, since dragon slaying hadn't worked out the way we thought, but she had to admit that she didn't have a plan for avoiding capture by Ivo.

I held my breath and hoped she wouldn't ask *when* we were going to go back, if not now.

I argued for research in a cloister library. Parz sighed. "Well, you were right, Princess. We need a lot more information. We need the *Handbook*. To Saint Disibod's Cloister, then."

"It seems the best choice," I said, my stomach asquirm with nervous anticipation. Saint Disibod's might very well be my future home. I was planning to ask the cloister to overlook my lack of dowry and take me in based solely on my family name and skills as a scribe. It was where I would reveal that I would not be returning to Alder Brook by Christmas, then say farewell to Parz and Judith.

"So we'd want to go up the Rhine and take the ferryboat to Confluence," Parz said. "It'll take us maybe a week to get there if we walk. Longer if—"

"I don't think I *can* walk that far," I said bluntly.

Parz nodded. "We agree." He pointed past me.

The silver mare was standing directly behind me, staring down at me with a piercing gaze.

"What? What do you want?" I asked her.

Judith had also already figured it out. "She wants you to ride her."

"I'm sorry," I told the waiting silver mare. "I can't. I can't ride you."

She flicked an ear at me.

"You can ride," Parz said.

"No, Parz. I can't. I've never been taught."

"Yes," he said gently, his voice quiet but strong in the utter silence. "It will be uncomfortable, possibly painful, but you can. I'll instruct you."

I hated him in that moment, for knowing my pain and asking me to meet it. But I gritted my teeth and faced the horse. She nickered at me. I held out my hand, and she nuzzled it. "I can ride you?" I asked.

She didn't say no.

Parz came around and boosted me to her back. I clutched the amethyst-and-sapphire pommel, thinking how this tiny portion of her saddle alone was worth a queen's ransom, and how it was the only thing that was going to keep me from death.

"Don't hold on to the pommel—hold on to her mane," Parz said. "If you start to slip, the mane will keep you on the horse; the saddle might want to slip just as much as you."

"Oh." I removed my right hand from its death grip on the pommel and lightly touched the mare's mane.

"Get your fingers in there. Pull it all you want—you

can't hurt her that way."

I knotted my fingers gently into her mane, then took my left hand off the pommel and did the same.

"Now, feet in the stirrups."

I slid my straight foot into the left stirrup. My crooked foot and the right stirrup, however, did not make so pleasant an arrangement.

"I don't know if I can," I said. "My . . . foot."

"The issue is the angle or the pressure?" Parz asked.

"Both."

"Then we will simply teach you how to ride without that foot in a stirrup, until we come up with a better way."

I was, as usual, embarrassed whenever any special attention was paid to my foot, but at the same time . . . I wasn't a sack of turnips. I was *riding*. I was riding the *silver mare*.

I grinned with excitement until it occurred to me: I was riding a horse of the Wild Hunt . . . alone.

Fear gripped my belly, and I clutched at the mare's mane.

"You're doing very well!" Judith called. Parz stayed at my side and put one stabilizing hand on my right leg.

"I'll catch you if you fall, so you don't need to worry," he said. "You ready?"

"Sure," I said.

"Judith, can you lead?"

The silver mare tossed her head and started forward, as if to prove she needed no one to lead her. She executed a perfect circle around the stable yard. Parz jogged alongside, explaining little things, his hand warm and comforting on my calf.

My head was a jumble, and everything was moving too fast—oh, not my mare, who was ambling along no faster than I went with a crutch, but the whole thing. *I'm not allowed to ride horses.*

But here I was.

By myself.

On a horse.

Alone!

I'd always been told I couldn't—and shouldn't—ride. I'd always been told I couldn't dance, either, and I'd nearly danced with Sir Egin the night before.

And, well! I had run away from my imprisonment at Snail Castle and joined up with a group of dragon slayers. A group that consisted of a failed squire and my handmaiden, but a group of dragon slayers nonetheless.

What else couldn't I do?

I wanted to go try everything immediately. I thought about pulling out a sword and riding into battle beside Judith and Parz, and almost laughed out loud.

"So, what's her name?" Judith called as the mare took me around the circle again.

I didn't answer.

"Tilda, what are you going to call her?"

"I'm concentrating!" I hollered. I was learning the things Parz was saying, about telling the horse where I wanted to go with my body's weight and small pressures and the reins.

"I think you have it," Parz said at last. "She's a smart horse, which isn't always a good thing for a new rider, but she's sweet on you, so . . . I think it will be all right."

"Now that you don't have to concentrate so hard, what's her name?" Judith asked.

"She hasn't said," I replied.

They both laughed, but I hadn't really been joking.

Parz understood, though, in spite of his laughter. "I think she'll let you know if you're wrong," he said, once his chuckle died away. "What do you want to call her?"

"Joyeuse." It meant "joyful" in the language of the northern Franks, and it was, in some ways, the word I'd been thinking since getting onto the mare's back.

An astonished and pleased look lit up Parz's face. "Perfect!"

"Why is that perfect—?" I began, and then

remembered that Parz loved naming horses after swords. I racked my brain. "Oh, yes. Emperor Charlemagne's sword was Joyeuse."

"And Sir Roland's sword was Durendal"—Parz's eyes swung toward the copper horse—"forged from the same steel."

"All right then," I said, and patted the silver mare. "How do you feel about the name Joyeuse, my dear?"

The mare snorted a little, and the earth suddenly moved up, down, and sideways rapidly. "What just happened?" I asked.

Parz and Judith were staring at me. Or rather, at my horse.

"I think your horse just danced," Judith said.

I tried not to look smug as I patted the mare again. "Joyeuse is clever like that."

"My turn," Parz said, wearing a devilish grin.

Judith shook her head. "Should I call in the bone-setter?"

"Not yet," Parz said, and attempted to leap onto the copper mare's back.

I never saw the mare move, and I guess Parz didn't either. One second Parz was halfway into the saddle; the next he was flailing and falling to the ground, and the copper horse was standing behind Judith.

And, hand to fire, the mare was *laughing*.

"Oof," Parz said in a tiny voice, face smashed into

the courtyard muck, and now I was laughing, too. I clapped my hand over my mouth, immediately chagrined and horrified to be laughing over someone who might be hurt. But Judith giggled as well, so hard she snorted, which made the guffaws burst forth uncontrollably from me. And beneath me, Joyeuse was still dancing with joy—and amusement?

Parz got to his feet, trying to wipe the muck and mud from himself, which somehow made us laugh all the harder. Judith tried to help him, but she was nearly incapacitated by her giggle-snorting.

Parz was not appreciative. "You laugh like a pig," he told her.

"I know!" she wheezed. "And Tilda laughs like a horse!"

"I do!" I said, and horse-laughed even harder. "Are you—are you hurt?"

"No," he said, and the sullen look on his face was almost enough to start us off again.

While Parz washed up in a bucket of water, Judith approached the copper mare with a slice of apple. The horse sniffed the air above her hand for a moment, then reached out with delicate teeth and ate the slice.

"Hi there," she said breathlessly. "Durendal? Can I call you Durendal? Will you let me . . . ?"

Some silent communication passed between them, and they went together to the mounting block, and

Judith clambered up into the high saddle. Durendal pranced back and forth a few times. "Tilda!" Judith called. "I'm—do you see?"

"I do see!"

A serious expression fell over her face, and she kneed the horse closer to me. "Do you—is it all right, Tilda? I mean, they both sort of belong to you, if to anyone."

I stroked Joyeuse's gleaming neck. "I'm telling you, they don't belong to me. This isn't my horse. I am her girl."

Judith nodded, a crooked smile stealing across her lips.

I watched Parz carefully when he returned from his washup, damp and still annoyed. His eyes flickered to Judith on the copper horse. But he wasn't angry, nor even jealous—*resigned* was the word that came to mind.

"Fine. I'll walk. I know when I'm not wanted as a rider."

I patted the silver mare between the ears. "Joyeuse?" I said. "Will you let Parz ride with me? We need to travel a long way."

Joyeuse tossed her head, but it didn't seem to be a no. A moment's hesitation, then Parz mounted up behind me—pillion, though. I was no sack of salt to be balanced in front of him anymore.

⚘

SIX HOURS LATER, I sat alone at the front of the ferryboat to Confluence, wedged between strangers. Parz and Judith were with the horses, being better able to stand for the whole of the voyage. When we arrived, I watched the maneuvering of the boat into its slip, occasionally glancing up to scan the crowds waiting at the docks.

That's when I saw Horrible Hermannus.

chapter 13

RECOGNITION AND FEAR WENT THROUGH ME LIKE an arrow.

Horrible was standing in the crowd at the edge of the ferry dock. I thought I must be mistaken, but then he turned and I was sure.

How could he be *here*?

"Oh, no," I moaned, rising to my feet and clutching the rails of the ferry tightly. I wondered if I was going to faint, but suddenly—a figure cut through the crowd, swirled his cloak around my shoulders, and turned me around abruptly so I no longer faced the docks.

"Th-thank you!" I said, stunned, and stared up into a handsome face I recognized from Upper

Folkstown. "Sir Egin?"

"Lady . . . Agilwarda," he said, his arm tightening slightly across my shoulders. He smiled down at me.

"Sir Egin! I wasn't expecting you on this ferry."

Sir Egin quirked his mouth at me, half frown, half smile. "My lands are across the Rhine from my liege lord's. Forgive me, my lady, but you look like you've seen the Wild Hunt."

Most people would have said, "like you've seen a ghost" there, and the odd turn of phrase gave me pause.

Sir Egin said casually, glancing over his shoulder, "There's a man on the docks looking right at you." All the strength went out of my knees with that, and I started to fall. Sir Egin caught me neatly.

"Stay calm," Egin said mildly, helping me reestablish my footing. "We don't know that he's seen you, whoever *he* is."

"I'm calm!" I snapped. I willed myself upright, willed myself likewise not to panic, or faint, or do any of the stupid things that it was occurring to me to do. For one thing, those actions were far, far beneath my dignity as a princess.

For another, there was absolutely nothing I could do about the matter, and losing control of myself would only make things worse.

"What's going on?" Egin asked softly in my ear.

"Why are you frightened of that man?"

"I'm not frightened!" I objected, though in truth, I was. I could think of only two reasons that Horrible Hermannus would be on that dock: he was working *for* Ivo and coming to take me back to Snail Castle, or he was working *against* Ivo and coming to take me back to Alder Brook.

Either way, he was taking me back to prison.

"I'd like to help," Sir Egin said. "Ride with me, back to my castle at Thorn Edge. I can protect you."

"Tilda!" Judith said, fighting through the crowd on the ferry. "Are you all right? Your face—"

"Don't look out at the dock!" I said, grabbing her good arm and spinning her around.

Sir Egin smiled at Judith. "Don't worry. I saw Lady Agilwarda looked unsteady. I came to her service."

"Yes—well . . . ," Judith said.

The boat finally docked. I drew my hood low over my face, and Judith grabbed my hand and pulled me away from Sir Egin, through the crowd to Parz. I lost sight of Horrible in the chaos, though I scanned the busy ferry slip constantly as we unloaded the horses.

Confluence was a proper city, however, and we were not going to be able to get out of it too easily. The eyes that the horses attracted were more than just envious—some of them looked angry and jealous.

We hurried out of the city, but not fast enough.

"We're being followed," Parz said.

My heart hammered in my throat. "Can we—can we outpace them?"

"On *these* horses?" Parz said, and now he was grinning. "If we can hold on, we can outpace them."

And outpace them we did. The mares required only the barest nudge before we were flying along the smooth Roman road south. Confluence was left behind, and, I prayed, Sir Hermannus with it.

"We need to disguise the horses," I said during our first rest break.

No one argued the truth of that; instead, we argued about how we were going to disguise them. In the end, we decided to use mud since there was plenty of that around, and some combination of leaves and torn-up clothing to disguise the rich saddles and tack.

I worried how the horses would react, but they seemed excited about the mud, taking the initiative to roll in it once we removed their tack and applied the first few fistfuls.

"So, we'll just be the youths without parents and *really dirty* horses, instead of the youths without parents and *jeweled* horses?" Judith asked.

I shrugged. We had no better options.

After our horses were sufficiently muddy, Judith and I went into the woods to pass water before we started off again. When we were done, she said, "The man on the docks who scared you. . . . Who was it?"

"I saw"—I hesitated just a bare moment before deciding to lie. If I told her I'd seen Sir Hermannus, she would never understand my running away from him. We might call him Horrible behind his back, but she'd never see why I'd try to flee from him. Not without realizing I was fleeing *all* of Alder Brook. "I saw Cousin Ivo."

"Ivo!" Judith gasped.

"I *thought* I saw him," I said quickly. "It wasn't really him at all. Nothing to worry about. We can just go on."

Judith's fear fled, but her anger remained. "I wish it had been him," she said, smashing her fist into her palm. "Between us and the horses, we could have made him our prisoner, taken him back to Alder Brook, and ransomed him to his own family."

I shrugged, thinking that unlikely even if I had seen Ivo in Confluence. "Cousin Ivo's parents don't have enough to pay a proper ransom," I said.

"Fine, then we make him clean the privies," she said, laughing a little—at herself, I think.

"Only seems fair," I said, though I felt sick to my stomach to be lying to Judith. I was going to tell her the truth in just a few short days, but not until we got to Saint Disibod's Cloister. She wouldn't worry as much about me once she saw where I'd be living, and she'd feel easier about leaving me there to go back to Alder Brook.

WE SPENT THE FEW hours before sunset convincing each other that we could afford both the money and the attention to spend a night at a guesthouse. Each of us in turn voiced doubts: Would the horses stay alone in a stable, all dirty? Would anyone bother the horses? Could we really spare the pfennigs to do this? And another one of us would counter the doubts: It looked like rain. We needed to buy food anyway. Tilda really needed a night inside to properly care for her foot (I was both irritated and grateful to Judith for saying that).

"We don't have that much money for the long term," Parz said. "Not unless we start managing to kill dragons and collect on their bounties."

"I'm not *actually* suggesting this, but one of Durendal's bejeweled mail mittens would be enough to keep us in fine style at the best guesthouse for a year," Judith said.

"That's assuming that Durendal wouldn't kill us for trying to nick her gear," Parz said.

We were silent a moment, watching the horses' ears twitch. None of us were convinced they didn't understand every word we said and speak human languages among themselves at night.

"Perhaps, eventually, a well-placed knifepoint could pry off a jewel in a sort of hidden area . . . if and when we need to," I said. "But for now, we have the rest of the reward money from Upper Folkstown."

We found a large guesthouse at a crossroads, reasoning that the size of the place would help us blend in. The common room was lively with the presence of a wandering minstrel, who sang a variety of songs. He alternated bawdy ballads with dreamy romances and heroic lays, which were the perfect accompaniment to pigeon stuffed with apples and prunes.

"Guess what?" Parz said, gnawing on his pigeon. "I heard from the landlord that there's a dragon living down near the town of Wood Ash, on the Roman road to Treviris. We have another dragon!" He eyed me. "Once we've done our research at Saint Disibod's, I mean."

I nodded, pleased he was still in agreement about the need for research.

I stuffed myself with bird and fruit, and listened with increasing joy to the music as it moved from romantic to funny to bloody, and thought I'd rarely had a finer time.

Then the minstrel sang the ballad about the hunter who falls in love with a swan maiden and steals and hides her swan feathers so that she becomes trapped in maiden form and marries him. Then she finds her feathers, turns back into a swan, and flies away. And the man dies of grief.

"I like that version," Judith said. "I always heard the one where the hunter goes looking for his swan wife after she flies off, and then when he finds her, he kisses her and she turns back into a woman. And then she just goes home with him again. That never made sense."

"Why not?" Parz asked.

"If she ran away as soon as she found her feathers, why would she go back with him?" Judith asked. "When he stole her feathers, she was basically forced to marry him."

"That's uncharitable," Parz said. "What if she loved her husband, but when she found her feathers again, she just got so excited she flew home? Like a pigeon. Birds have a powerful sense of home."

"Have you considered," I said, "that maybe the swan maiden just wanted to make her own decision? Maybe she did love him, but the chance to make a choice was too much to give up."

"Hmph," Judith said. "If I could transform into a swan, I'd never give up my feathers for a husband."

Parz leaned forward to spear an uneaten prune off my trencher. "I like Tilda's idea. Maybe she didn't give them up. Maybe once he realized she chose him, he could return her feathers so she could come and go as she pleased."

I smiled at Parz, and he smiled back, munching my prune.

"I don't care what you say, I like the one where he dies the best," Judith said, and when Parz opened his mouth to reply, she shushed him. "Hush, he's starting the next song!"

I pushed back from the table, not so much full as no longer hungry. I was like the swan maiden, wasn't I? Running away because I'd found my feathers. Maybe Judith would forgive with me if I explained it to her that way.

chapter 14

I LAY IN BED NEXT TO JUDITH, RESTLESS, SLEEPLESS; Parz snored on the floor beside us. I couldn't sleep, no matter how hard I imagined the pleasures of working and living at Saint Disibod's Cloister, with a desk in the scriptorium and a reassembled writing box. Dark clouds kept intruding on my fantasy, until I turned my full attention to what was bothering me.

As we drew closer to Saint Disibod's, I couldn't avoid some hard truths. Come Christmas Day—or maybe sooner, when it was clear to her that I wasn't going back to Alder Brook—Judith was going to leave me. Even if she wanted to stay, she couldn't. By rights she belonged to Alder Brook. By rights, on Christmas Day, Alder Brook owed her a new dress and her season's pay. I wouldn't have either of those things to give her then, anyway.

I couldn't imagine life without Judith. It was not a simple matter of having no one to rub my foot or help me dress. I could do those things myself if I had to. I had a few hazy memories of the time before she became my handmaiden, but even then, I had known her since I was born. Her parents had served my parents since *they* were all young together. Judith might be my servant, but we had also grown up together. Gotten in trouble together. She was my friend—she was my family.

But nuns didn't have personal servants, did they? Certainly not ones they couldn't afford to pay out of their own purses. And I couldn't feed Judith without Alder Brook. She might love me as much as I loved her, but she couldn't stay in the cloister.

I'd been so thoughtless. I'd failed to see that my new life wouldn't include Judith. I could forgive myself for not seeing it, though; when I told myself I didn't need anyone else . . . well, it was hard to forget that Judith wasn't a part of me. When she left, it would feel like chopping off my foot. And not my crooked foot—the good one. The one I never paid attention to because it wasn't always aching and holding me back, even though it was the foot I really couldn't do without.

And I was chopping off so much more. Frau Oda was a piece of me, too, with her mustard poultices. She had been so proud of my learning, even as she scrubbed ink from behind my ears and under my nails. Somehow, I'd forgotten about Frau Oda, and how much she loved me.

And Judith's parents, Aleidis and Ditmar, and Father Ripertus, who taught me to write, and Wortwin the Robust who carried me everywhere when I was younger, and—

I bit my lip, hard. Alder Brook was better off without me. Wasn't it?

In the morning, I told myself, *I will tell Judith I'm not returning to Alder Brook. Then there will be no going back.*

When the others woke in the morning, I felt ancient and ill.

"Did you not sleep well, Tilda?" Judith asked after Parz left to give us some much-needed morning privacy.

I opened my mouth to tell her the truth, but my courage drained from me so quickly that maybe I'd never had any at all.

"Where did you get that necklace?" I asked instead, pointing at the small chain I'd noticed in Upper Folkstown.

Judith reached back and unfastened it. "Parz made it from horsetail hairs," she said.

I stared at it. He'd woven the hairs around each other in such a way they looked like a chain made of silver and copper wires. "It's beautiful," I said, and felt a small surge of jealousy that Parz would have made it for her but not me. I forced the jealousy away angrily: Judith was a handmaiden and not used to receiving many gifts. And she was true to Alder Brook, where I was false. Did she not deserve it more?

WE GOT BACK ON the road. Parz rode with Judith to give Joyeuse a break, not that she *appeared* to need it, and Durendal seemed patient with having two riders now. The travel was easy as long as we stayed on the Roman road; but even though all roads lead to Rome, eventually one has to go in the wrong direction. We started down a dismal, gully-washed road that barely deserved the name, and travel got much slower, even for horses of the Wild Hunt.

"Let's go to Wood Ash," I heard myself say. "Let's go slay the dragon there."

Parz turned to look at me, eyes very blue as they caught the sunlight. "What about the research?"

"This *is* research," I said, almost frantic. I didn't want to go to Saint Disibod's. I didn't want to have to tell Judith I was abandoning Alder Brook. Not—not yet. We had time before Christmas.

"Are you sure?" Parz asked me, but exchanged glances with Judith.

"We have the horses now," she said.

"Yes," I said. "We have the horses now."

WE RODE THROUGH AUTUMN drizzle and fog for three days, until we arrived at the village of Wood Ash and found a guesthouse. We stabled the horses and went inside to ask the landlady about the dragon and a room for the night.

Sleep was elusive for me once again.

My mind wandered. I thought over all the saints' stories I'd read about dragons. It was never entirely clear if the dragons ate the maidens they were given, or just . . . sort of . . . converted them to evil. Or made them scrub floors. Maybe that's all that really happened: lots of floor scrubbing.

I finally slept a little and woke before dawn, eyes like pits of sand. Rather than disturb the others, I hobbled down to the stables to see the horses.

The rain had rinsed away more of the mud than was good for their disguises, but it seemed to me that on the day of their first dragon fight, they should not have to wear dirt. I crept into their stalls and brushed each one down as Parz had taught me, trying not to be melancholy when I thought about never seeing the squire again after I joined the cloister.

As I worked on Joyeuse, I kept catching sight of the silver saddlebags hanging from the wall. When I finished her grooming, I sidled over to the bags. Just a peek.

I lifted out one of the mail mittens and slid it onto my hand. It fit perfectly. I flexed my hand, feeling strong and tough. I dug deeper into the saddlebag, came out with the fine silver linen coif, and slipped it over my hair. Also a perfect fit. I took up the mail shirt next, and again, perfect.

I stood there for a long moment, feeling the weight and heft of the armor. It wasn't heavy. It felt right. You might have thought randomly acquired mail that came with a horse escaped from the Wild Hunt would be meant for a large man, but it fit me exactly.

Then, with a sigh, I slid back out of the shirt and coif and mitten and put them all away.

Joyeuse had grown excited when I put on the armor, and she didn't lose the excitement now that I'd changed out of it. Every jingle of the mail had made her hop from foot to foot. I calmed her by petting her so-soft nose and feeding her apple slices.

Knowing how much a warhorse could eat, and faced with the destruction of entire vineyards at Upper Folkstown, I had been worried, early on, how much feeding the Wild Hunt horses would cost us. But much to our distress, neither of them wanted anything but the handful of fruit we gave them on a daily basis. At first, Parz had told us to be patient: horses in new situations often lost their appetites. But there was nothing about their attitudes that suggested they were uneasy, malcontent, or unsettled. Or hungry. They didn't like people, but they seemed to enjoy spending time with us. And they always ate apples and grapes when offered.

They never seemed to lose any weight or become fatigued. They both slept like normal horses, Parz assured us.

"Well, my friend," I whispered, "do you want to go fight dragons?"

She struck a silver hoof against the wall.

"I'll take that as a yes."

"Tilda?"

It was Judith. She pulled out Durendal's saddlebags, and I helped her dress.

The copper armor fit her perfectly, just as well as the silver had fit me. I frowned. Two sets of armor cut for girls? The Wild Hunt's leader was a woman, but . . . Not all girls were alike. Judith was broader, taller, and more buxom than me. How did her armor and my armor both fit so well?

"Magic armor, I guess," I muttered.

"What?" she asked, smoothing the mail shirt over her hips.

"Nothing," I said, not wanting to admit that I had tried the armor on; I was never going to wear it into battle, so it seemed vain and hopeless and, well, just silly. "Is it heavy?" I asked, even though I knew the answer: No, it wasn't heavy, it was perfect. When I'd worn the armor, I'd felt strong and safe in a way I'd never felt before.

"Not heavy at all," Judith said, and then left the stall to execute a cartwheel. She looked as surprised as I did when she regained her feet. "I think I'm spoiled for all other armor."

I gave a half twist of a smile, trying not to envy her. It wasn't that I wanted to fight in a battle. Far from it. The thought of facing down an opponent and being struck, and worse, striking back, actually nauseated me. It wasn't just my foot that held me back from fighting. It was my nature first; I couldn't imagine myself holding a sword with the intent to kill someone. Even a dragon.

I opened the stall door for Joyeuse—which was a joke, for at this point, the mares had proved that they only stayed in stalls as a courtesy to us.

Joyeuse and I went outside to wait for Parz, who disappeared into the stable. We had decided that, since Durendal had more or less chosen Judith, Parz would use Joyeuse to fight.

Parz came out clad in the silver armor, and I stared.

"I thought you wouldn't mind," he said, forehead wrinkling, his charming sidelong smile fading.

"I don't. The armor fits you so well. . . ."

Parz plucked at the mail shirt. "As though it were made for me." He came over, carrying the silver sword and silver belt. His mouth and brows were straight lines of seriousness.

"Will you gird me, Princess?" he asked, and knelt down to offer me the sword and belt.

I had seen my mother do this for various knights who owed our family service. She had done it for my father the day he left on his fateful pilgrimage. It was strange to do it now for Parz. But I did it.

I took the sword belt and bade him stand. I reached around his hips and girded the belt on him, saying, "With honor, and with bravery." At this point, my mother would always kiss the knight on the cheek.

I hesitated. The thought of kissing Parz was enough to make me blush so hot that I might turn into a candle, so I just kissed the air beside his cheek. Even then, I couldn't look at him right away.

"Ready?" Judith asked, coming out of the stable, also holding a belt. For a moment, I thought she was going to ask me to gird her, too, but I had already done so in the stable, just with less formality and ritual.

But then I noticed this wasn't a belt, but rather a gem-studded girdle, one of the treasures from

Joyeuse's baggage; threaded onto it were a silver dagger and a leather pouch. Judith grinned, girding the belt around my waist before I had a chance to react. She kissed my cheek and said, "The pouch holds two pens, a knife, and a horn of ink. We know better than to go into battle and leave our scribe unarmed!"

"Where did you get these?" I asked, peeking into the pouch.

"Parz and I sold the necklace he made out of the horsetail hairs to the innkeeper here."

"Ready?" Parz asked. I didn't say anything at all, being too overcome by their thoughtfulness to speak. I just accepted his help into Joyeuse's saddle.

And then we were on our way to fight a dragon.

WE TURNED OFF THE road after a short league, onto a narrow path through a large stand of young, slender pines.

"This is it," Parz said, catching sight of a half-burned, half-eaten carcass of a cow lying in a field.

"I'm going to dismount here, then," I said. Parz helped me down from the horse and then climbed onto Joyeuse's back. She tossed her head a little, but settled in. I tried not to be jealous that she didn't buck him immediately off.

I busied myself with pulling out the *Handbook* and my new pen pouch, even as I wondered if this was a safe distance from which to view the fight.

The only hint we had of what was coming was the shadow that crossed the sun. The stink of sulfur stung my nose, and an undulating green-and-red-scaled wall passed overhead, almost close enough to touch. The wall slid from view, and I realized the wall was the passing belly of a great flying beast. A gigantic tail slid away over the trees, leaving behind only blue sky.

Dragon.

chapter 15

By the time I caught my breath, the dragon was gone—and so was everyone else. Both horses and their riders had plunged into the trees after the dragon.

"Swine!" I swore, shoving my pens back into the pouch. "Swine, swine, swine!" I jammed my crutch into my armpit and hobbled off as fast as I could go after them.

I wasn't sure how long I walked. Time never seems to flow the same when you are late for something, and I was *very* late for something. Roars and screams rose from not so very far away, and the air filled with the acrid scent of smoke.

I entered a burned-out clearing from the west. On

the south side of the clearing a cave mouth gaped. Joyeuse stood guard near a copse of trees at the far edge of the clearing, tensely scanning the sky.

It took me a moment to realize that the pile of silver at Joyeuse's feet was Parz's supine body.

Joyeuse gave a high-pitched whinny when she saw me.

My heart was in my throat, but I decided that Joyeuse was not the sort of horse who would guard a dead body. Or so I told myself in the long moments before I reached them, when each footstep seemed like the death toll of a church bell. Where was Judith? Where was Durendal?

"Parz?" I called, hurrying to him as fast as I could.

He was breathing, but unconscious.

"Good Lord!" I cried, chafing his hands and wrists as I inspected him for signs of damage.

Parz coughed, blood bubbling between his lips.

I nearly screamed in terror. My life in Alder Brook, far from any battlefront or disaster, had in no way prepared me for this kind of injury. I couldn't think of how to stop him from coughing, but I could imagine the blood running back into his lungs and choking him. I slid my hands up underneath him and pushed, getting him over onto his side so the blood could drain from his mouth.

"Please don't die, Parz," I heard myself saying,

and my voice was so strange. I realized I was crying. "Please, Parz. Please. You can't die. Oh, I'm—" I paused for a sob, which I tried to stifle against my shoulder. "I'm being so silly, I'm speaking such nonsense. See how bad it is, for you to be trying to die on me like this? See what it's doing to me? So. Just don't die!"

Parz stopped coughing, and for a moment, I was horribly afraid he'd also stopped breathing. And I guess he had, for he was summoning together a great gob of blood. I yelped when he raised his head, turned it, and spit the blood gob out into the grass.

"You're alive!" I shrieked.

"Think so," he rasped. He looked around, his gaze barely focusing. "Where's Judith?"

"I don't know! Are you all right? What's . . . Something's broken, what's broken?"

He looked thoughtful. "Everything," he croaked, dropping his head back to the ground.

"Can you get onto Joyeuse's back?"

"Not even," he said, and groaned.

I ran my hands over his arms and legs, trying to figure out if anything *was* actually broken. I couldn't tell. I just didn't have the training. "I'm afraid I don't even know how to move you."

He shivered. "That's all right. Don't really want to move."

I unclasped my cloak and threw it over Parz's body. I couldn't think of what else to do—he was shivering so hard, it seemed the right thing.

I bit my lip when I heard a distant roar and the screams of an angry horse. "Parz, where did Judith and Durendal go?"

"Judith—never—came out of—the cave," he said, teeth chattering between each phrase.

I looked at the dark cave mouth. "Did you go in there with her?"

"Yeah. Came out—before the—dragon."

"And then, what, you all fought the dragon?"

"Wasn't much of—a fight. Dragon was—so big."

I had seen that for myself. The dragon heads mounted in Sir Kunibert's hall had ranged in size from a large dog's to a regular horse's. None of those dragons could have been close to the size of the great beast that had flown overhead earlier.

That flew overhead *now.*

The hum in the air from the noise of the dragon's wings shook me to the soles of my feet. Joyeuse stood beside me, and we watched as the dragon sidestepped into the cave, hissing and roaring the whole way.

I moaned. "Judith."

I bent down and gave Parz the kiss on the cheek I'd failed to give him during the girding. "Quickly—anything I should know about using a sword?"

"The sharp part goes in the dragon," he said. "Wait—" He grabbed my hand. "You can't go in the cave. Too dangerous."

"I have to go."

He struggled to rise. "You're going to undo my greatest act of chivalry if you get yourself killed."

"What, rescuing me from Snail Castle?" I didn't have to push his shoulder very hard to get him to lie back down. "Surely you've done something more chivalrous than that."

"Not . . . yet."

"Stay down," I told him. I ordered Joyeuse, "Guard Parz."

The silver sword lay nearby. I snatched it up. Sword in one hand, crutch under my arm, I faced the dark mouth of the cave alone.

chapter 16

THE DRAGON BURST FORTH FROM THE CAVE'S mouth, roaring the whole way. I fell backward as the creature winged up, over my head.

I had one glimpse of a small, dog-sized dragon on its back before it disappeared beyond the trees.

Was it carrying a . . . baby?

I stood up slowly, testing to make sure I hadn't injured something when I was bowled over. I noted with distant clarity that my hands were shaking. I resettled my crutch.

A human scream came echoing out of the cave. Judith's scream.

She was still alive!

"Judith?" I called.

No answer.

No answer, and no choice. I was no warrior, and yet . . . here I was, facing darkness with nothing but a sword.

I swallowed down my fear, and gripping my borrowed sword, I entered the cave.

I froze for a moment, blinded by the darkness after the bright autumn day, and afraid that I'd suddenly fall down a large hole in the floor if I tried to move forward in the dark.

But gradually my eyes grew accustomed to the dimness, and I could make out a faint, flickering light ahead. A lantern? Parz had a lantern; had he taken it into the cavern and left it behind?

For perhaps the only time in my life, I wished I were left-handed. Even though that would make scribe work nearly impossible, I would not now be in the position of trying to hold a sword in my distaff hand. My right arm was occupied with my crutch.

I shouldn't be here. I'm not a fighter. I'm certainly no dragon slayer.

No. I wasn't a dragon slayer, but I was a princess, and one of my people was ahead of me, in the dark and alone.

I inched along the rough cave floor toward the flickering light, listening for anything, any sound from Judith, any dragonish noise. I stopped myself from calling her name no less than three times, but when I rounded a narrow curve and came out into a wide cave and saw her lying in a heap next to a lantern, I couldn't stop myself.

"Judith!"

Immediately, a hissing and spitting creature that waggled its neck like a goose came charging from the shadows. I lifted my sword before me, and it must have caught the light just right, because the dragonet darted away and back into the gloom. The shadows writhed and scales glimmered—and I realized there was more than one dragonet hiding in the dark.

Judith said nothing, and I feared the worst. I crept along to the lantern, not taking my eyes off the shadows from where the dragonet had come.

I didn't want to speak and risk the dragonets' attentions, so I nudged Judith with my toe.

She sat up immediately, and I breathed a sigh of relief. She'd only been playing dead. I pointed back the way I came.

She shook her head, and pointed at her leg. I assumed she'd broken it, and stooped awkwardly to feel her thigh, trying to assess the damage.

But instead of a break, I put my hand in something warm, wet, and sticky, and Judith screamed when I touched it.

The dragonets screamed back—great, honking

bleats that filled the cavern till my head rang. I clapped my hands over my ears, shouting, "Can you walk?" while I tried to make sure the dragonets weren't advancing on us.

"I don't know!"

"Try! On the count of three!" We counted, and I levered her up. She leaned on me too hard, so I stuck the crutch in her right armpit and slid my shoulder under her left. I needed the crutch for stability as much as anything, and even leaning on me, Judith could provide that.

I still held the sword, which left no way to carry the lantern. We had to abandon it and make our way out of the cave in darkness, with the dragonets milling in the shadows behind us.

"No choice," I grunted, taking the first dragging step forward toward the cave mouth.

"*Shhh*," Judith hissed almost silently in my ear, and squeezed my ribs painfully.

We took another staggering, dragging, hopping step forward, then another. Judith grunted, and now I squeezed her ribs. She stopped grunting.

It seemed like the longest walk of my life, but I was sure that once we reached daylight, the worst would be over.

When we reached the cave's mouth, though, the worst was *far* from over.

The big dragon was back, circling overhead, its enormous wings sending gusts of air down that made my ears pop. It opened its mouth and bellowed out a stream of flame at Parz.

But Joyeuse and Durendal were both there now. Joyeuse made an unnatural sound of anger and Durendal's nostrils and eyes were wide with fear, but nonetheless, the mares turned sideways against the flame. They caught all of the dragon's fire with their bodies. When the flames hit, their bodies turned from silver and copper to glowing orange.

I only realized I was screaming when I ran out of breath. I felt ready to vomit, sick with grief and terror. I buried my face in my upper arm, unwilling to see the horses die so horribly.

But even as I hid my eyes, I realized that I wasn't hearing what I had expected to. There were no screams of anguish. I lowered my arm and found Joyeuse turning to track the dragon as it circled again, while Durendal pawed the air.

The horses and Parz were unburned. The mares' bodies and tack remained the orange-red of heated metal, but nothing was charred except the waterskins that we'd left tied to their saddles.

The dragon sent another flare at Parz, and again the horses turned to take it on their sides. A gout of flame licked underneath Joyeuse's belly, igniting the grass. But Durendal stomped her hoof, kicking up a shower of blue-green sparks that cleanly and quickly burned the grass out—and the fire was gone almost as soon as it started.

The dragon circled again, looking for a better angle of attack, I thought; the trees protected Parz on one side, and the horses protected him on the other. The treetops, however, would not *remain* cover if the dragon ignited them.

I thought for certain that this would be the dragon's next move; but it must have spotted Judith and me, for it landed in the clearing, facing us, touching down one delicate claw at a time as its great wings backstroked the air.

The dragon turned its long, snaky neck toward us, making a variety of hissing and popping noises, punctuated by low moans and high-pitched growls. It snapped enormous jaws at us.

I inched Judith leftward, trying to get us away from the cave's mouth so that the dragon could pass us and enter the cave.

The dragon snarled, and with the snarl came orange fire. It licked toward us, and I shrieked as the heat rolled over us. I buried my face in the crook of my arm.

Judith said, "Get behind me."

"What? No, you're injured!"

"*Get behind me*," she roared, shoving me back. The dragon vomited forth another great gout of fire, and, screaming, I buried my face in Judith's neck, even as I was terrified that she was cooking inside her shell of heated armor.

"Stop it!" I shouted, popping up behind Judith when the fire blast ceased. "We could have killed your babies and we didn't!"

"Tilda!" Judith cried. "What are you doing?"

"Just—just let us pass!" I said to the dragon. "And we'll leave you alone to get your babies!" I shouted over Judith's shoulder when the flame died away. "We don't want to hurt you! Not anymore!" I dived right, trying to pull Judith after me. She came, and we both hit the ground and rolled farther away.

We had landed under a bush. Judith slapped out some incidental fires on her body—mostly from a kerchief that had been tied around her arm. I sighed in relief. She was well enough to care about that little tiny fire.

The dragon sidled toward the cave entrance, still hissing and growling anytime Judith or I twitched. But neither of us was getting up, between her wound, my foot, and the fact that my crutch now lay in the dragon's path.

We watched in silence as the dragon turned and sang into the cave. A moment later, the last two dragonets zipped out. They flapped their wings fervently, trying to take flight. The larger dragon—their mother—tucked her nose underneath the chest of one of the dragonets, then flung it behind her and onto her back, between her wings.

She did the same thing with the other dragonet, and then she launched herself into the air.

The dragon circled once and flew away.

chapter 17

JUDITH HAD BEEN ABLE TO RIDE AFTER THE DRAGON left—but just barely. Parz refused to try to get on a horse, and I couldn't blame him; but when I suggested lashing two stout branches together to make a stretcher pulled by the horses, he said he thought walking would be the least painful option. But he couldn't make the distance, and in the end, we ended up devising the stretcher.

With any other horses, I might have given up long before we reached Wood Ash again; I might be living still in a forest clearing without them.

There was no bonesetter in Wood Ash, and the midwife who came to see about our injuries insisted on sending an appeal to Saint Disibod's Cloister for help with Parz and Judith. The cloister sent one of its famous healers, a Sister Hildegard, to assist us. Within the week, we were all in good enough shape to remove to Saint Disibod's proper.

All three of us ended up in the infirmary. Parz had broken ribs and a broken arm. Judith's wound was deep and had to be watched closely for infection.

I had emerged largely unscathed from the fight with the dragon, except I'd lost my eyebrows and eyelashes. But there was always the matter of my foot.

The infirmary was a marvel. It had a small, stream-fed fountain, lush plants grown in pots, and every kind of herb and gem and metal. The infirmarians constantly sang songs of Hildegard's devising that were supposed to aid in the healing of both spirit and mind.

Sister Hildegard began an intensive regimen with my foot right away. "This is not recent damage. This is an innate injury, developed in the womb," Sister Hildegard said during the examination of my foot. "You'll forgive me if I stop calling you Lady Agilwarda, yes?"

"Um, just Agilwarda is fine," I said.

"I was thinking more of calling you Mathilda," Sister Hildegard said, and carefully placed my foot on the floor.

"Wh-why?"

The nun looked at me acutely, as though she saw through my flesh to the shape of my bones. "You're Mathilda of Alder Brook," she said. "The lost princess."

I gaped. "Yes," I said cautiously. "I am Mathilda."

Sister Hildegard smiled. Her white veil and wimple were almost blinding. "The cloister received word that you had gone missing. We have been praying for you daily, that you did not fall into villainous hands."

"That's nice," I said feebly, all good manners abandoning me.

"We're pleased to have you, and to help you. Now . . . I'll just go fetch flour, animal fat, and eggs."

"To eat?"

Hildegard laughed. "No. They're for hardening bandages." When she returned, she gave me a long, painful session of stretching, then heat treatments, and then followed it by wrapping my leg in bonesetter's bandages with a splint, and coating them in her mixture of items from the kitchen.

"When this dries, it will align your foot faster than just stretching alone," she said.

"Am I—is my foot going to be normal?"

Hildegard shook her head. "If we had gotten to you when you were an infant, perhaps. But even so you will be able to walk a little better by the time your friends are healed from their injuries."

THREE WEEKS LATER, I no longer dreamed of a peaceful cloister life.

It turned out that at Saint Disibod's, I had no more time to attend to the *Handbook* than I would have had at Alder Brook—in fact, I had less time, between my treatments and the daily work of the cloister. And the interruptions to pray were near constant. I had made the mistake of telling Hildegard I was contemplating a life of religious devotion. Judith and Parz, as secular patients of the infirmary, were not expected to follow the nuns' schedule. I was awakened in the middle of the night to pray and read scripture. Then I was sent went back to bed, only to wake at dawn and begin needlework, which was hourly interrupted by prayer.

I began to dream of a writing desk in a remote cave, far from any nuns or monks. With, perhaps, a mute servant to do all the heavy work, to bring me food and empty my privy pots, and to mix my ink.

What little time I spent in the library was excellent, though.

I got to look into a copy of a book by Pliny, one of the heathen natural philosophers I'd only heard of; I also found a bestiary that cataloged all species of serpent from basilisk to boa to dragon. But the most thrilling thing at Saint Disibod's was a book I'd never expected to read, Isidore of Seville's *Etymologiae*. It was supposed to contain practically everything that it was necessary to know about everything.

I paged through the volumes of *Etymologiae* eagerly, but with thoroughness. There were many fascinating subjects in it, including a note scrawled in the margins about how wearing specially gathered succory plants could turn you invisible.

My hand itched as the idea came to me: Wouldn't invisibility be a great tactic for fighting dragons? You could just sneak into their caves without them seeing you, and *slice-stab*: dead dragon. Like Siegfried hiding in the ditch at Drachenfels, but with much less mess.

The *Handbook* took shape only slowly, even though Sister Hildegard helped me with the organization of the book and the sorting of important information from random facts. She was no simple healer, being a fine musician and singer as well as a writer. We talked most often at night, when I found myself burning candles to read when I should have been sleeping, and after she finished her nightly rounds in the infirmary.

"What have you learned today?" she always asked, and I would tell her.

"What about invisibility?" I asked, and showed her what I'd copied down about succory plants.

She glanced at my copy, and rattled off six other ways to turn invisible.

"Wait, wait!" I cried, writing as fast as I could. "A

tiny horn filled with turnsole . . . What was that about mistletoe? And fern seeds?"

She repeated herself patiently until I had written it all down. "Of course, dragons have excellent senses of smell," Sister Hildegard said, watching me write PLANTS WHICH CONFER INVISIBILITY across the top of the list. "And excellent hearing as well."

My pen faltered. "Invisibility isn't enough, then."

"Perhaps not. What other ideas do you have?"

I shoved the useless invisibility list aside and flipped through the *Handbook*. "Most of the stories I find have some saint-in-the-making just defeat the dragon by being holy enough. Trying to make Parz holy isn't an entirely lost cause, but . . . Well, I'm beginning to think that dragons aren't all evil. Maybe. Do you know? Are they?"

"Are all hawks evil?"

"Of course not."

"What have you observed of dragons that would make you believe they are evil, that you have not observed in a hawk?"

"I've not observed very much of dragons at all," I said slowly, assembling my thoughts. "But from my direct observation, I have only seen dragons protecting their homes, or being good parents—protective, like a swan with her cygnets or a hen with her eggs."

"I have observed the behavior of many animals,"

Hildegard said. "And I've seen no instance where an animal acts from pure evil. But I have seen men who are selfish, men who rob the world of beauty and joy for the sake of pride and vanity, men who scorn duty to follow their own pleasure."

I nodded, looking down at the book. I closed the cover softly and traced the binding. "Women, too," I said softly. I cleared my throat. "Perhaps this handbook is folly."

"Why do you say that?"

"Maybe we shouldn't be killing dragons at all. They're just animals, and we can't, or won't, even eat them. That's wasteful, and a sin."

"When they threaten our crops and herds, what then?" Hildegard asked.

"Birds threatened our crops, and we put up scarecrows," I said.

"What about when dragons threaten our maidens and children? Don't people require and deserve protection?"

"Sure," I said, in agreement but frustrated. "But who can tell when it's a true threat? Who makes that call?"

"Well, isn't that part of being a dragon slayer? Like a knight who determines when to joust and when to leave the field. . . . Isn't there a measure of judgment in dragon slaying, as in all things?"

I felt so stupid. Of *course* dragon slayers did not just go around killing every dragon they ever heard of. They weren't trying to wipe out the whole race of dragons. Sir Kunibert had had a contract for every single one of his kills.

It was thoughtless and irresponsible of Parz, Judith, and me to blunder around, thinking all dragons were evil and needed to be destroyed, when we didn't know the first true thing about dragons.

I thought of the Wild Hunt. What had the Hunter said? I hadn't thought it very important at the time, but now . . . now I felt it most keenly, and it stung: *Ignorance does not make the wrong choice into the right one.*

IT WAS HARD TO speculate who was most bored with our time at Saint Disibod's—Parz, Judith, or the horses. Another reason I had so little time to work on the *Handbook* was because if I didn't visit the horses twice a day, they would free all the other horses. They didn't even have to kick the doors down; they were experts at opening latches with their teeth and lips. What was worse was that they started teaching the cloister's horses how to do this, too.

Judith was bored, but she had also been in service since the age of seven, and there was a part of her that I think enjoyed lying in a bed and letting others wait on her. Some of my free time had to be spent entertaining her. I tried to hit two flies with one slap by reading to her from my day's work on the *Handbook*.

Parz amused himself by weaving more of his horsetail-hair necklaces, carving whistles out of tree branches, and asking the monks about bookbinding. Once he was healed enough to be out of bed for long stretches of time, he came to watch me work on the *Handbook*.

I was copying down the story about the dragon that the Roman emperors had kept chained in a pit to eat Christians. That story didn't have a helpful ending at all; Saint Sylvester had just descended into the pit, preached at the dragon a bit, and then sewn a cross into the dragon's lips, which utterly incapacitated it. But I copied it anyway.

The flame on my candle flickered as Parz came into the room. He looked down at my work. "I don't know how you manage to do that without mistakes," he said.

"Concentration," I said. "Practice. And understanding the price of new parchment."

"It's a talent," he said, hooking a stool with one foot and dragging it over to sit beside me.

I could feel the heat from his arm next to mine, he was so close. Back at Alder Brook, I would have been delighted with this. Back at Alder Brook, I would have let my thoughts drift to the daydream that he would take my ink-stained hand in his. Right now, it just seemed like an interruption. I had hardly any time in the library.

But I showed him what I'd written. "Can you imagine a dragon letting you sew its mouth shut? I think this might be a fabrication."

Parz shrugged. "If it's written down, it must be true."

I laughed then. I could not help it; my horse laugh burst unprincesslike from me like a sneeze. Parz looked puzzled, like a cat who has been swatted in the nose for trying to eat the Lenten fish.

"I cry your pardon," I said. "I did not mean to laugh in such a manner. It's just that I have copied manuscripts, and have spent time with monks who have copied their whole lives. I have made mistakes, and I have seen mistakes, and I have copied things that make *no sense*, and I do not believe that writing things down makes a lie or a mistake any truer than if it was just spoken."

"Sure, but . . . ," Parz said, and ran his finger down the margin of the book. "But this is in *Latin*."

"Tilda," he said after I was done laughing at him. He reached into the pouch at his waist and held out a coiled necklace of braided silver and copper tail hairs. "I finished making this for you."

I leaned forward to touch the necklace cupped in his hand. "It looks like proper chain. Even more so than the necklace you made for Judith."

"Here," Parz said, and held the necklace by its ends. I turned my back and scooped my hair out of the way. I must not have gotten it all, though, because his hand brushed my neck before he started knotting the ends of the necklace together. I felt myself flush slightly, and stared ahead. I was used to servants helping me dress—but only female servants.

"Thank you," I said, touching the necklace where it lay against my chest.

"Tilda?" Sister Hildegard poked her head around the corner. "You have a visitor. Father Ripertus?"

"Father Ripertus?" I was shocked. "How did he . . . ?"

"The abbot wrote to let your priest know you were safe."

"He did *what*?"

Sister Hildegard's face was gentle but implacable. "A perfectly rational thing to do, when a dispossessed princess shows up on the doorstep. Did you think we were going to keep it a secret?"

chapter 18

"FATHER RIPERTUS!"

My teacher looked older but still kind, still wise. Seeing him provoked such a wave of homesickness that I almost sat down on the flagstones of the receiving room.

He held open his arms and swept me up in a big, woolen, incense-scented hug. "We were so worried!"

I pulled back, not sure what to say to him, or how.

His eyes swept over me, from the cast on my foot to my chopped-off hair. "You have been busy, haven't you?" he asked mildly, and brought me to sit down next to him on a bench.

"I—I—" I didn't know where to start. I also didn't know what to tell the truth about. But if he'd had a letter from the abbot, there was no telling what he knew.

It's probably a bigger than usual sin to lie to a priest, anyway.

So, proceeding cautiously, I told him everything that had happened since I'd last seen him. Well, almost everything. Though it was on the tip of my tongue to mention it time and time again throughout the story, I did not reveal the important fact that I no longer wanted to be the Princess of Alder Brook.

"And then we ended up here," I said. "Parz and Judith are all but healed. And I'm . . ." I shrugged, not knowing how to finish that sentence.

I waited for Father Ripertus to say something.

"I'm disappointed in you, Mathilda," he said at last. "Dragon slaying? How reckless! How foolish! I understand the others sustained injuries, and well-deserved ones. Parz, perhaps, learned a little caution from his. And Judith, perhaps, learned that bravery is no substitute for experience. But what injury did you sustain, Tilda, that could teach you what you need to learn about responsibility?"

His words stung. "I know plenty about responsibility," I said. "And I have had *plenty* of injury to deal with through my life."

"You are a liege lord, and you have a duty to those who follow you. Even so far from Alder Brook, you are still a princess," Father Ripertus said. "You have done poorly for Parz as his friend by letting him run around the countryside—but what you have done to Judith?"

"Judith *wanted* to come! She *wanted* to slay dragons!"

"Many people want many things, but it is your *duty* as Princess of Alder Brook to give people what they *need*, not what they want!"

"Well! Isn't it fortunate that I will no longer be a princess after Christmas Day! I'll be no one's liege when Alder Brook passes to Ivo!"

Father Ripertus looked grim, but before he could speak, Judith hurried into the room. "Father Ripertus, Tilda, don't argue. I'm sorry I persuaded Tilda to come play at dragon slaying before we came back to Alder Brook, but it seemed like the best way to stay clear of Ivo—"

"I'm not going back." I stood. "Ever. I'm letting Ivo have Alder Brook."

Judith gaped. "You can't give up like that! Ivo doesn't just get to win—"

"I'm not giving up! I'm doing what's best for Alder Brook. They think I'm cursed. They think I can do nothing for Alder Brook. And I can't! I told Ivo when he kidnapped me, he could have it!"

"Well," Father Ripertus said heavily. "And I thought Ivo was lying about that."

Judith's eyes widened with disbelief. "Then . . . then why did we rescue you?"

"I never asked you to rescue me!"

"So that's it?" Judith cried. "You just give up on your duty, you abandon Alder Brook and turn your back on it?" Judith asked.

"But I don't *want* that life!" I said. I didn't know *what* life I wanted, but I still said, "I want to become a nun. I want to write books. I can't write at Alder Brook. I want to write like Boethius."

"Father Ripertus just told you! I heard him! It's your duty to deal with *need*, not want, and you need to rule Alder Brook—and Alder Brook needs you."

I dashed away angry tears, unable to explain any of the thoughts whirling around my head. My father had left Alder Brook, hadn't he? He hadn't let his duty to us stand in the way of his plans for the Holy Land—why should I be any better than him?

But how could I think that about my father? He had died a hero . . . hadn't he?

When I didn't respond to her, Judith turned to Father Ripertus. "I don't care what she wants *or* needs anymore. I'm leaving. I'm going home. I know *my* duty. May I travel with you, Father? I'm well enough to go."

"If we still have a home to travel to, child, then yes." He turned to me again. "Ivo is selling off every movable possession he can—linens, furniture, clothing, books, dishes, silverware, dogs, horses. . . . And when Christmas Day comes, and you are not there to assert your claim, he will bequeath Alder Brook to another lord and join his retinue."

"But why?" I exclaimed. Alder Brook's free status was its only true power. Its prince had no masters but God and the emperor.

"Ivo has been promised a very large number of gold marks for his allegiance," Ripertus said. "And gold is its own stepping-stone."

"Of course," I muttered. "Greedy pig-hound."

It would be like an earthquake, to start thinking of my future as Princess of Alder Brook again. I didn't want to. So many things had hurt me there. I had learned how to wear ice on my face and iron over my heart there.

But I had been trying to believe I didn't care about Alder Brook. I had tried to believe it was just a place: the place I'd been born, the place I'd lived, the place that my father had left.

And I had tried to believe I could leave it, too. Without a backward glance, like my father. I had gathered this coldness close and tight within me.

"There's more," Father Ripertus said. "Ivo is punishing those who speak against his rule."

"Who?" Judith burst out. "Who is he punishing?"

I thought about Judith's parents suffering under Ivo. The cold, mean spirit within me drained away, thinking about Aleidis and Ditmar in danger.

"Oh," I said, in a tiny voice.

Ripertus rubbed his nose. "Sir Hermannus was put in the stocks for three days."

"Why?" Judith asked.

"First, for protesting the sale of Alder Brook's allegiance. He was told if he did not recant his protest, he would be put to the ordeal of boiling water. But second, because he disappeared for days, looking for Princess Mathilda."

So, it really had been Hermannus I'd seen at the ferry dock! I'd begun to think I imagined it.

"Poor Hermannus!" Judith cried. I stared at her, my mind in turmoil.

"He recanted, right?" I said.

Ripertus shook his head. "He did not. He faced the ordeal, and plucked the stone from the boiling water."

We were all silent. "Is he all right?" I whispered.

"God was with Sir Hermannus, and his wound was healing, not festering, when I examined it ten days ago; however, that has not changed Ivo's mind, and now Hermannus is in the dungeon."

I had thought Hermannus would provide an important check on Ivo's ambitions, but that hope was gone. Ivo was destroying Alder Brook.

No one wanted to become some other principality's second-best holding, to be drained by extra taxes and fees, to face losing sons to constant warfare. Alder Brook had a long history of relative peace; we guarded our borders but stayed out of most local conflicts. My father was the first ruler of Alder Brook in generations to feel the urge to fight, and he took only volunteers and traveled far away to wage war. Not that our people had been pleased by that choice, either—far from it.

"My own protest has remained limited to coming here," Father Ripertus said, almost drily. "Someone had to remain free."

"Did anyone else get the ordeal?" Judith asked.

"No. All of the other protesters recanted, against their consciences," Ripertus said. "But at my counsel."

"I thought . . . Ivo would be better for Alder Brook," I said slowly. "I thought . . . he was uncursed, uncrippled. . . . He'd find a wealthy wife and save Alder Brook."

"He thinks of nothing but his own desires and comfort," Ripertus said. "He is no true prince."

There was an awful, squirming moment of silence, and I knew Ripertus and Judith were both thinking that *I* had thought of nothing but my own desires and comfort.

It was what *I* was thinking, anyway.

And it was true. Horrible Hermannus had served Alder Brook better than I had. Far better.

I was frozen in a deadlock of shame and guilt and horror, and a strange sort of tenderness for Hermannus, too. I had no idea what to feel, let alone to say or do. I stared at the floor, thinking hard.

The silence was broken by Judith's fury. "Say something!" she shouted. "You could harden butter in your armpits, you're so cold!"

All the times I'd looked away from people's spite, I had just turned away so they could not see how much they hurt me—time upon time upon time. I had never been cold, never! Not once. And how could Judith, of all people, not know this truth about me? I stared at her, wounded.

"That's enough, Judith," Ripertus said. "You know Tilda better than that. She does her hurting on the inside, not the out."

I was so grateful to him in that moment that I wept, face buried in my hands.

It was so unfair, so very unfair, for Judith to accuse me of this coldness, when it was Alder Brook and its inhabitants who had caused it; it was my duty to accept their fear and dislike.

Wasn't it?

The earthquake inside me started low in my feet

and belly. The memories of all the bad things that had ever happened at Alder Brook were not in isolation; there was also the memory of all the times I'd been praised for a just decision or a wise notion. There were memories of all the people who had loved me and tried to make me feel better in the face of the ignorant and idiotic. Frau Oda. Father Ripertus. Judith's parents. Wortwin the Robust . . .

Judith.

It was hard to remember those times—hard to remember them and let them be as important in my memory as the hurts and slights. But I had to remember them.

And I had to accept that maybe my memory wasn't perfect. I couldn't even recall when I'd started calling Sir Hermannus "Horrible," but I would always remember this day, the day I learned of the ordeal he suffered for the good of Alder Brook. I would remember it for the rest of my life.

I was born a princess, trained from my earliest life in duty and how to care for Alder Brook. Ivo's two good feet were no substitute for that training in how to rule, or how—or when—to curb his own ambition.

I lowered my hands.

"I'm sorry, Judith," I said, and it was as clear and as simple an apology as I had ever considered.

"What does that mean?" she asked, her voice still

raw with anger and tears.

“It means that it’s time to go home to Alder Brook.” It was time to give up my wild ideas about freedom and writing a great book. It was time to save my lands and my people.

chapter 19

WINTER WAS COMING. I COULD SMELL IT IN THE air as we rode quickly away from Saint Disibod's Cloister. Heavy gray clouds in the west seemed to say, "All wise souls should now be home."

It was just now dawning on me how unwise I truly was.

And how selfish.

I kneed Joyeuse parallel to Durendal. Parz was riding pillion behind Judith, but there was no hiding my selfishness from him, so I started to talk.

"I know an apology isn't enough, Judith. But I'm sorry. For everything. But especially for not telling you I didn't want to go back to Alder Brook. I'm going back to make it right."

Judith looked straight ahead. "You don't deserve to be the Princess of Alder Brook."

Parz's jaw dropped.

"I know," I said. "But it's what I have to do, nonetheless."

Now Parz looked everywhere except at me. Judith didn't take her eyes off Durendal's ears.

Judith said, voice low, "I wish you had felt like you *could* tell me. I never . . . I never knew you wanted anything else."

I bit my lip against a prickling of tears. "You have to understand . . . I thought Alder Brook hated me. Wasn't it the right thing, to give them a chance to have a prince they could want?"

Judith turned. "No, of course not!"

I blinked. "How not?"

"You're the ruler that they want! They just don't know it. Yet."

"Judith, I'm not even the ruler *you* want."

She put her hands over her face for a moment. When she put her hands down, she tried to smile. "That's not true."

"You just said I don't deserve to be the Princess of Alder Brook—"

"I spoke in haste, all right? It's not like anyone *deserves* it. It's just luck, the luck of how you're born."

"It truly is," I said, and tried a smile.

She smiled back.

Grinning now, I looked over at Parz. He met my glance with wide eyes. "I didn't hear *any* of that," he said.

"You didn't?"

"Nope. Chivalry occasionally causes deafness."

It wasn't that funny, but we all laughed, relieved to still be friends and in each other's company.

Behind us, Father Ripertus coughed. I flushed. I'd forgotten we weren't alone, for a moment. I thought back over my recent behavior, trying to pick out which things I'd said that were unsuitable or indelicate for a princess. . . . But then I decided: I was a princess anyway, whether I was occasionally poorly behaved or not.

THE NEXT DAY WE reached the Rhine, exhausted and aching and hungry.

Well, the humans were exhausted, aching, and hungry, and so was Father Ripertus's horse. The metal mares, of course, were as lively as young chicks.

When we'd departed, I had not really considered money. We still had a few pfennigs. And I'd thought Father Ripertus would have some money, but he'd fled Alder Brook in the night and, when he found me, had assumed *I* would have money.

Our notion that we could pry a few jewels loose

from some piece of the armor or tack proved false. The horses' possessions were practically indestructible. As for selling any of it—truth be told, we were all more than a little afraid to do so. We slept in barns and ate windfall apples, but the more apples I ate, it seemed the hungrier I became.

"We're going to sell the silver girdle today," I said to the others as we rode into the town of Bingium Bridge. "That's just the end of it. We're selling it. To the richest person in town, because . . . well, there are a lot of jewels in this girdle."

But when we inquired around the town, it turned out the richest person around didn't live in town. "You might try Sir Egin at Thorn Edge," I was told.

Sir Egin! I remembered that name. He had offered to help us before. Surely he would give us a place to sleep, perhaps provisions for the road. I vaguely recalled Judith didn't like him, but she was too hungry to protest. We turned the horses north to Thorn Edge.

The sun was just setting when we climbed the mountain to Egin's castle. I had only to give my horrible fake name—Lady Agilwarda—to the porter, and we were invited in. Judith was sent to the kitchens to eat, while Father Ripertus, Parz, and I were given a brief tour of the castle—though I think we all wished we were lowborn enough to get sent to the kitchens, too, on that particular day.

Thorn Edge was beautiful. I had not expected it to be so, a toll castle perched high above the Rhine. The castle commanded a long view of the river both north and south. Across the river were vineyards and forests, and behind the castle, forest climbed the mountain to the sky.

But the true beauty of the place lay in the terraced gardens at the center of the castle. Even this late in the year, a few valiant flowers bloomed, sheltered from autumn wind and frost by the walls.

"Lady Agilwarda!" Sir Egin greeted me with a smile. "And her friends. It's . . . Lord Parzifal, is it? Such an unexpected delight! And I do not know you, Father."

"Ripertus," my old teacher said with a bow.

I stared at Egin, struck dumb by the changes in him. I had remembered him as so handsome and charming, but I could see that—yes, he was still handsome, by the letter of what handsomeness is—but everything about him repulsed me. There was a cold, fishlike deadness behind his eyes, and it made my skin crawl.

"I'm sorry," I said, backing instinctively toward the stables where Joyeuse and the other horses patiently waited. "I think—I don't wish to intrude."

"Nonsense! You came to me—you must have a reason!"

"I—we just . . ." I didn't know how to explain what we needed without appearing incredibly vulnerable, which, of course, we were.

"We have a long journey," Parz said. "Lady Agilwarda needs provisions and a place to stay for the night, I'm afraid."

I listened with despair to Parz's ramble of lies and truth, and stared at Egin. *How did I find him so lovely before?* I wondered. I remembered whirling about with him, and being interrupted, and the brief expression of dark anger that had crossed his face. And Judith's calm voice informing me that Egin had just buried his seventh wife.

I had forgotten all that, on the ferryboat.

How had I forgotten that?

"I assumed you would stay the night," Egin said.

Father Ripertus and Parz eagerly agreed, before I had a chance to refuse.

"Good, good. Let me show you to Thorn Edge's private rooms, that you may refresh yourselves before supper." We followed him into a squat tower, up a circular staircase. I struggled to keep pace up the curving stairs.

Egin showed Parz and Ripertus into a warm, wood-paneled room with a crackling fire, which they exclaimed over before he closed the door behind them. Then he guided me up another two turns of the tower stairs before showing me a pleasant-enough chamber. It held a low bed piled with soft silk pillows and fur covers, a well-appointed fireplace, a little table, and an ornately carved stool. A narrow window overlooked the great river.

I surveyed the place, then turned back, trying to smile.

"It's rather plain, I know," Egin said.

I glanced at the lush tapestry on the wall over the bed. "It's quite lovely."

"It needs a woman's touch. The whole castle is in need of a proper mistress."

I blinked. He had just buried his seventh wife. How much of a mistress did it need?

"Well," I said, "it looks fine to me."

"No, no—the only true ornamentation in this room is—you."

It was just too much, but what could I do? "It'll be fine for one night," I said, hoping that if I implied that I agreed with him, he'd leave off the conversation.

Sir Egin looked stricken. "Just one night? I had hoped you might grace Thorn Edge much longer than that!"

I frowned. "I have urgent business."

"Oh, how urgent can it be? You are such a young lady. You can't have any great responsibilities yet."

I wished.

But I thought it would be unwise to let him in on my true identity, so I just smiled. "I do not mean to be rude, but perhaps I could have a little something to eat?"

"Of course!" Egin said. "I'll leave you to freshen up, then come on down to dine."

"Yes, I should like to change my clothes," I said. "Can you send my servant and my bags?"

"I'll send a servant right away."

A SERVANT CAME, BUT not Judith; she carried a stack of lavender-scented clothing, but not my saddlebags.

She introduced herself as Frau Dagmar and told me that she had been the handmaiden to the previous lady of Thorn Edge. Then she said little more, except to insist she would help me change my clothing into what Sir Egin provided.

Frowning but trying to remain gracious, I changed into a soft robe of orange-tawny wool. Frau Dagmar removed the long necklace that Parz had made for me, feeling it did not go properly with the outfit, as I needed a brooch to close up the neckline of my dress.

I laced on the mantle. Then, for the first time in weeks, I donned a circlet over my veil. It felt strange to have something resting on my head. By rote, I went to arrange my braids, and had to pause when they were not there.

Frau Dagmar led me downstairs to a hall that should have been full of retainers but held only Sir Egin. He bowed to me, and I thought, *Perhaps he looks best in candlelight,* for it seemed the full force of his handsomeness and charm had returned.

I couldn't remember why I'd thought him uncharming upon my arrival, in fact.

He explained that Father Ripertus and Parz had elected to dine privately in their room. "But we shall not feel their absence, I'm sure," he said.

Supper was elaborate: pressed venison, spiced pike, meatballs presented as golden apples, and tiny roast piglets stuffed with bread, eggs, nuts and currants. For sweets, there were yellow jellies and eggshells blown out and stuffed with marzipan. A bowl of almonds and a bowl of coriander sat before our shared trencher, supposedly to taste between courses, but I abstained. They called coriander "dizzy-corn" because it made the head spin, and it seemed my head was already doing plenty of that, between Sir Egin's fantastic stories and even more fantastic compliments.

He asked me to tell the story over and over, of how I "trapped" the metal mares and faced down the Wild Hunt. The telling and retelling and retelling the sequence of events made me dizzy as well, until the details started to blur together.

Egin walked me to my bedroom door and bent to

kiss my cheek good night. I entered the room and shut the door behind me.

The quiet *snick* of a key turning gave me pause.

I'd been locked in.

chapter 20

THE STRANGEST PART OF BEING LOCKED INTO MY tower room was that I didn't care. *Oh, it's probably to keep me safe,* I thought, untying my mantle and falling into bed.

In the morning, after I washed and dressed, I tried the door again and found it locked.

Right. It had been locked the night before, too. Hadn't it?

I shook the door harder, in case it was just sticky. But no, it was well and truly locked.

I sat down at the little table and waited.

Not much later, a key rattled in the lock, and Frau Dagmar came in, accompanied by a pair of younger handmaidens. I sat still as they emptied my night pot, aired my bedding, and built up my fire.

"Where is Sir Egin?" I asked finally.

"Around," Frau Dagmar said, shaking her keys at the handmaidens, as if this would make them move faster.

"Can I see him?"

She jangled the keys slower, peering at me over her nose. "What for?"

I blinked at the keys, considering. "Isn't . . . isn't it odd that my door was locked this morning?"

"Very."

I frowned. I watched the handmaidens, trying to remember exactly what it was I had been planning to do that day. "Can you send my servant Judith to me?"

"She's resting."

"Can I see my friend, Lord Parzifal?"

"He's also resting."

"Perhaps my confessor, Father Ripertus, could come to visit me?"

"He is"—she paused—"*resting.*"

"Could I have my saddlebags?"

Frau Dagmar shrugged. "I don't see why not. I'll bring them to you. If you—"

"If I what?"

She spun the keys around, then caught them in her fist. "If you promise not to mention to Sir Egin that you have them."

"Am I not supposed to have them?"

The handmaidens had paused in their work and stared at Frau Dagmar. Now she jangled her keys at them again, and they scurried back to action.

"Why is the door always locked?" I asked.

Frau Dagmar whipped her ring of keys at one of the handmaidens, just missing her. "Get out of here, you two! Out! And never speak of this!" They ran, and she kicked the door shut behind her.

She stared at me, eyes burning. "I am not your jailer, Lady," she said. "Remember that. No matter what happens, remember that."

I stared at her, frightened. I wasn't even certain what I'd said. "I'm sorry," I said.

Now she stared at me pityingly. "You seem smarter than the others," she said. "But not by much."

I frowned. "I'm smart enough," I said.

"Oh? And how did you get imprisoned in Thorn Edge, then, if you're so smart?"

I opened my mouth to object that I wasn't imprisoned! But then I thought about it. I thought about the locked door, and how I hadn't seen Parz or Judith or Father Ripertus since we'd arrived, and my dizziness, and her keys.

Thinking about it was like wading through honey.

"I wasn't brought here against my will," I said slowly. "But . . . I can't leave, can I?"

"No," Frau Dagmar said. "And you're not the only one who can't leave."

"My friends? They're imprisoned, too?"

"Well, they *are*," she said. "But that's not what I'm saying. There are many prisoners here."

I squinted at her. What did she mean?

"You—you're a prisoner, too?" I asked.

"I—I—" She started to speak, but the words seemed to strangle her. She clutched her throat.

I stared at her and clutched my throat too, trying to figure out what was happening to her. My fingers reached for my horsetail necklace but didn't find it. I'd forgotten to put it back on.

"Shouldn't have spoken," Frau Dagmar wheezed, her face turning purple. "God have mercy on you, maiden!" She staggered over to where her key ring had landed and fell to her knees when she bent to pick it up. She dragged herself upright and heaved herself out the door. "Remember what I said!" she croaked. "I am not your jailer!"

I stared at the closed door for a long moment.

The key turned in the lock.

I blinked. When was Sir Egin going to visit?

I SPENT THE NEXT quarter hour looking for my horsetail necklace, and found it half under my bed.

I put it on.

Immediately, it felt like I had uncrossed my eyes. Or surfaced from rinsing my hair too long in the bath. Or stopped holding my breath until spots hovered in my vision.

Sir Egin was wooing me. Sir Egin intended me to be his eighth wife.

And probably—one had to assume—he was going to kill me.

Because a man didn't just end up widowed seven times over. Not one as young as Sir Egin. He had to be killing them. But why?

I paced the tower room, tried the door a few times, and wondered what was being done to my friends.

When Frau Dagmar brought me my dinner, I asked, "You've served at Thorn Edge for a long time, have you?"

"All my life. Sir Egin hasn't always been master here, though."

"You've probably seen a lot of weeping maidens at the castle since him."

"Most don't weep. Most are pleased to marry him. He's a charmer. The only ones who weep are the ones who haven't met him yet. You'll see."

I shivered. It was bad enough to dread the marriage, to dread my likely death; it was worse to dread the thought that I might welcome it.

"I hope I won't see," I said, and my finger traced

the line of my necklace.

"I didn't bring your bags," Frau Dagmar said. "I didn't have a chance."

I shrugged. It had been a lot to hope for. The *Handbook* would have been a nice distraction; as it was, I was nearly going out of my mind with worry. I was going to be married and killed soon. And I had no idea whatsoever what was happening to my friends. I was afraid to ask after them.

I paced the room, looking for weaknesses. I thought of a hundred ways to escape, and a thousand reasons none of them would work. The biggest problem was this room. The door was too thick, too well made; and the hinges were on the other side. The windows were impossible—even a baby wouldn't have been able to slide out those narrow slits.

I would ask for the liberty of the grounds, then, and see if I could figure out a way to climb over a wall. Or maybe there was someone I could bribe. Or maybe—

Maybe it didn't matter, until I got out of the room.

I paced some more, until my foot tired.

I had absolutely nothing else to do. Nothing to read. Nothing to write on—not permanently, anyway. I might have asked for some sewing, but by God, I wasn't going to thank Thorn Edge for my imprisonment by supplying them with darned stockings.

Pretending I wanted to sew might give me some weapons . . . well. Sewing needles. They were probably too smart to leave me scissors.

I gave up on sewing and counted the boats plying the Rhine.

That grew boring in short order, so I practiced my penmanship with a splinter from the kindling and soot from the fireplace, on the surface of the small table in my room. I'd write out rows of even letters in perfect minuscule. My favorite practice was writing out the declension of *minimus*: *minimus*, *minimī*, *minimō*, *minimum*, *minimō*, *minime*. . . . The pattern of the downstrokes in the *m*'s and *n*'s and *i*'s was soothing and regular.

It was a strange way to wait for one's doom, I knew, but what choice did I have? I couldn't seem to pray. I could tear my hair, weep, and cry. But that wasn't in my character. I was a princess. Every time I was tempted to cry, I thought of new words to practice writing in soot.

Mostly, I tried not to think of Parz or Judith or Alder Brook, and how badly I was failing them.

It was easier that way.

ONCE MORE, SIR EGIN seemed less handsome, though his hair was still as bright and he was still as tall. His pleasant appearance in the doorway of my chamber didn't make me like him any better, though.

His smile was full of toothy charm, and he bowed gracefully to me. "A pleasure to see you again, Agilwarda," he said.

"I'm too young to marry you," I said bluntly.

"On the contrary! Girls your age get married all the time, and to men much older than me."

"The contracts may be signed between men and girls in those situations, but we both know that the marriages are not true ones until the girl is older," I said. "And I don't think that waiting is your intention, since you'll just kill me in the end, like the rest of your wives."

Sir Egin's charming smile twisted into an expression cruel, cynical, and deeply entertained.

"Further," I said, "I do not consent to this marriage."

"I already have consent, Mathilda," he said, reaching inside his purse to pull out a scroll that dangled with seals. "Straight from your cousin's hand."

My jaw dropped. "You know my name."

"I know your name," he agreed. "After we met for the second time, on the ferryboat, and you were so frightened of the man you saw, I took the time to discover who you were. . . . Imagine my surprise when I visited Alder Brook and met your cousin—he so easily consented to our impetuous marriage! It seems he finds you inconvenient."

"Our 'impetuous' marriage—and when is that going to take place?"

"It's lucky to marry at the dark of the moon," he said. "Just a few days before Christmas. It is the perfect day for our wedding."

"I've never heard that the dark of the moon was lucky before." I frowned, perplexed. What was this game?

"You're very young," Sir Egin said. "You've not heard of a lot of things."

And he left.

Once he was gone, I practically fell onto the bed, deflated and defeated.

FRAU DAGMAR BROUGHT MY saddlebags the next day.

"Oh—thank you!" I exclaimed. "Thank you, thank you, thank you. . . ." I pawed through the first one, and then the second, looking for the *Handbook*. It wasn't there. "There's something missing," I said.

She shrugged.

"Why aren't you speaking?" I asked.

"He can't take all my words," she said. "Just the—" and she stopped with an abrupt choking noise. She coughed for a long moment, then tapped her throat with her forefinger. "Just the important ones."

"I'm missing a book," I said. "Smallish, handbook-sized . . ."

"A book," she said. "You're a reader, then?"

"Of course."

She shrugged. "Haven't seen a book. Sorry."

After she left, I went through the saddlebags again, hoping against hope that I'd find the *Handbook* folded into a dress or something. But there was nothing.

I kicked the bags and sat back down at my table, disgusted and annoyed.

I thought about the croaking and choking when Frau Dagmar was about to say certain things. "He can't take all my words." Was she was under a spell? Did Sir Egin have that kind of sorcery at his command?

What had he done to Judith, Parz, and Ripertus to keep them quiet and subdued—the same spell? Or set of spells? I thought about my behavior the first night, how I had accepted so many things he'd said, and not thought twice about things that had seemed so urgent. . . . It had been like a fog cast over my mind. How much time had passed in that fog, before I—?

In the distance, I heard a neigh like a silver trumpet. It wasn't terribly far. It was within the castle.

Joyeuse.

I had to get to Joyeuse.

I leaped out of bed, stumbled on my bad foot, regained my balance, and tried the door. Just in case.

Locked.

I went back to bed and put my head on my knees, threading the long horsetail necklace through my fingers.

I lifted my head and stared at the necklace.

Could it be the *necklace* that stopped Sir Egin's enchantments?

chapter 21

"TELL ME AGAIN THE STORY OF HOW YOU TRAPPED the metal horses," Egin demanded the next day.

I deliberately set the necklace down on the bed beside me, to where my hand would naturally fall if it weren't in my lap. Then I laced my fingers together and looked at Sir Egin.

I smiled fatuously at him, suddenly so pleased to be in his company. "It was Saint Martin's Eve. We were sleeping in a barn up in the vineyards. We heard a great roaring noise, and the whole barn began to shake—"

"Skip to the horses. What did you do to the horses to make them notice you?"

I couldn't stop smiling. "I stopped them from trying to kill Judith," I said. I felt like the world was blurry behind him, and he was the only thing truly visible to me. "When we are married, will this still be my bedroom?"

"What? No. Tell me about the iron bridles again."

"Well, I wanted to take the bridle off, and so I asked Judith how, and she told me how, and then I took it off—" My hand dropped to the shiny necklace that lay beside me on the bed. Immediately, the sense of blurriness faded. I shook my head. "And I—and eventually I—sorry, what was I saying?" I clutched the necklace and decided I was done with the experiment.

"About the iron bridle," Egin said through gritted teeth.

"Right. You know, being trapped in this room is bad for my leg."

He ignored that. "When you met the other horses of the Wild Hunt, did they seem interested in you?"

"I'm going to limp a lot on our wedding day if I don't get some time to walk outside."

"I don't particularly care about your foot," he said.

From any other bridegroom, that might have sounded loving.

He pounded his fists together, knuckle to knuckle, then lifted them to his mouth and bit them. I stared at him. “Tell me about the Hunt,” he whispered.

“Well,” I said thoughtfully, “it’s hard to remember it all when my foot hurts so badly from inactivity.”

“I would have thought inactivity was the proper treatment for your foot,” he said.

“Not according to Sister Hildegard,” I said, which was mostly true.

He smiled. “Fine. I grant you the freedom of the inner garden for two hours a day. Enjoy it. It’s about to snow.”

“Thank you,” I said with quiet calm, as though my heart did not sing at the thought of being closer to freedom.

“Now. Tell me about the Wild Hunt. Tell me about the Hunt leader.”

Emboldened by my success, I added, “I also want to talk to my confessor, on my walk.”

“Gaugh! Fine! *Tell me about the Hunter.*”

So I told him. Again. His face was closed and scowling, no matter what I said. I couldn’t figure out what details he really wanted to focus on, or why, but he’d had me talk about my meeting with the Hunter more than any other part.

He stalked around my small chamber as I described the moment again. He heard nothing to his particular liking, and stormed out.

❧

Frau Dagmar showed up about an hour later, and she guided me down to the garden. When I skidded on frost-slicked flagstones, she grasped my arm with both of her hands, holding me upright. Before we broke apart, she passed to me under the cover of our cloaks an oilcloth-wrapped package, just the right size and shape to be the *Handbook*. Then she nodded to me.

Moving as stealthily as she had, careful that no one watching us should know what I had, I slipped the book inside my robe and enjoyed how it felt pressed against my ribs.

I walked around the garden, holding tightly to the stone walls. Sir Egin was not wrong—snow was coming. A chill wind bit my cheeks, and the trees thrashed restlessly beyond the castle wall. The world smelled rich with earth and fresh with snow. I took a deep breath and despaired. Winter was no longer on its way—winter was *here*. It made escape even more unlikely and infinitely more difficult.

I strove to stay upright as I wandered farther into the garden. Eventually, I made it to the edge of the wall overlooking the drop-off, but instead of gazing down at the steep, forested hill that lay between the castle and the Rhine, I faced the garden gate.

"Tilda?"

I turned at Father Ripertus's voice, unable to

believe it was really him. We embraced.

"Are they treating you all right?" I asked.

"Sir Egin is a delightful host!" Father Ripertus said.

Oh, no. Father Ripertus was enchanted. Like I was when I didn't wear the horsetail necklace.

A trio of squirrels ran toward us, playing a game halfway between chase and follow-the-leader. The two lead squirrels veered off nimbly when they approached me, but the one in last place stopped, confused, then tried to go two ways at once. I laughed a little, noticing this squirrel was much smaller than the other two. A late-born baby, perhaps? But not a baby any longer—Judith and I had raised a squirrel from blind, pink puphood on goat's milk, and this was no pup. She was about half grown—my age, in squirrel years.

The squirrel shook her fuzzy little tail at us thrice and ran off, over the garden wall and up into a small window. The squirrel chattered—and then I heard Joyeuse respond with an interested nicker.

The stable was right there, behind that wall!

"Father Ripertus, take my arm. I want to go over toward that gate. . . . Careful, the stones are slick."

Ripertus guided us to the gate that led into the stable yard. "Joyeuse?" I called.

With a noise like an earthquake, Joyeuse destroyed

the stable wall. Shining like the Christmas star, my horse bounded over to me and knelt.

Another earthquake, and out popped Durendal.

Neither had their saddles. I swung onto Joyeuse's back with ease born of need. I yanked at Father Ripertus's robes, shouting at him to mount the horse with me. Whatever Egin's enchantments were, the horses were immune and made us immune, too; as soon as Father Ripertus touched Joyeuse, he was yelling in my ear, "Go!"

Joyeuse rose to her feet and we were practically airborne, she took off so fast over the low garden wall to the courtyard, across the courtyard to the castle gate.

A mass of men-at-arms was forming up before the gate, facing this way and that, seeming not to know where the threat was coming from, just that there *was* a threat. Durendal dived into the knot of men and started kicking indiscriminately. There were cries of pain, and I buried my head in Joyeuse's neck.

I thought Durendal would kick down the castle gate for us—what couldn't these horses kick down, after all?—but the spiked iron portcullis must have been too daunting, because the next thing I knew, Joyeuse was in the air, leaping *over* the gate. I was holding on with just my knees and fingers, and I really couldn't scream long enough or loud enough to fully exhibit my terror at finding myself so high in the air on Joyeuse's back. Father Ripertus's arms clutched my waist, and his screaming was even louder than mine.

But then we were on the ground, and Durendal was beside us. The horses ran out into the forest. Behind us, in Thorn Edge, hounds bayed and men shouted. A clamor rose—warning bells, hunting horns. I leaned backward and urged Joyeuse down, down, down toward the Rhine.

chapter 22

WE'RE FREE. I WANTED TO SHOUT IT ALOUD, BUT I was keenly aware that it would be a very short freedom if I did not spend every moment of it wisely. And if I did not hold on very, very tightly.

The horses dashed between the trees almost as if the trunks didn't exist. Not a single branch brushed us in our passing, Joyeuse was so adept at weaving in and out even in her headlong rush. She leaped a stream; I nearly screamed as my rear end came off her back for a long moment, even though it was as nothing compared to the leap over the gate. Then we were down again, as lightly as a bird landing to catch a worm.

We crossed a path, then another path. The horses jumped a fallen log, then bolted over a road. And then we skidded to a halt at the narrow, stony beach of the great river.

The Rhine flowed with winter sluggishness, though it was hard to see the thin floes of ice that churned up to the surface. It was still faster than any other river I'd seen.

Father Ripertus gasped in my ear. "We have to get to Alder Brook!"

"Yes—get down, take Durendal. Tell me—Parz and Judith?"

"Both alive and well, last I saw them," Ripertus said, sliding to the ground.

My sigh of relief came out a little ragged, and I closed my eyes. "All right. Alder Brook. Horrible is our only hope now." Even in the thick of things, Father Ripertus had time to give me a disappointed look for that nickname.

Joyeuse's ears scanned the forest. Castle Thorn Edge perched high above us, and I could see no activity near it—but the trees obscured much. I strained to listen.

Father Ripertus climbed creakily onto Durendal's back. "Are you ready?"

"No—we're splitting up. Egin is going to come after me. He wants to know something I know about the Wild Hunt. Don't wait for me. I'm going to try to draw him off. Get to Alder Brook as fast as you can. Make sure Horrible—Hermannus, I mean—ransoms Judith and Parz from Egin. And me, too, if I get recaptured."

"But Tilda—"

"Go!" I shouted.

I think he might have argued more, but Durendal listened to me, not him.

I leaned low over Joyeuse's neck. "Let's give Egin the chase of his life, love."

She wheeled to the left and we pelted back up toward the castle, while Durendal and Ripertus headed north.

We had been under way for less than five minutes when Joyeuse seemed to pivot on one hoof and whisked us in a new direction. Moments later, I heard dogs baying behind us. We had been about to run into an ambush.

"Dumbhead!" I muttered beneath my breath. Joyeuse's ears flattened. "Me, not you," I said. "I should have been expecting that!"

Joyeuse was fast, but the thickness of the forest slowed her, and the hounds remained close on her heels. The noise of our passage and the yelping of the dogs obscured any other sounds, and I couldn't tell how many humans and horses pursued us. Then the sound of a hunting horn filled the air, low and dulcet and frightening.

We were on the path upward, away from the Rhine, and the sounding of the horn seemed to come from all around us. Was it ahead or behind? I couldn't tell. I panted in fear, in time with the bellows breath of the running horse beneath me.

"Whoa, whoa, don't go this way, that's back to the castle." Joyeuse slowed but didn't stop. The baying of the hounds grew closer.

Ahead, in the trees, for one brief moment, I saw Sir Egin sitting atop a nervous bay horse, horn in hand. He saw us—and blew three short blasts. The chorus of hounds behind us grew louder; another horn echoed Sir Egin's in the distance.

Joyeuse spun downhill.

In moments, Joyeuse and I were back at the shore of the Rhine. We paused at the river's edge. "North or south?" I asked. Had Durendal and Father Ripertus put enough distance between us to make it safe to follow them? I couldn't see how.

South then.

I turned Joyeuse upriver and we flew along the Roman road for several long breaths—until I saw him ahead of us.

Sir Egin.

From the forest up the mountain, a stream of hunting dogs poured.

Not south, then. And not uphill, either. And I

wouldn't lead them north after Father Ripertus.

That left one direction. "Into the river," I whispered, and Joyeuse turned instantly, rushing down to the rocky shore once more. I twined my fingers in her mane and held on.

Joyeuse did not hesitate. She plunged into the icy river.

Frigid water poured into my boots, and I sucked a scream in backward. The water rose to my knees, and pain shot through my legs. I turned my head and buried my teeth in the fabric of my cloak.

But there was no rethinking this. I could only hope that we wouldn't be swept apart by the current. If I lost Joyeuse . . . I would die. I wove my fingers tighter into the horse's silvery mane, wishing I had reins to tie around my wrists.

Then I remembered the *Handbook*, tucked inside my dress. It had an oilcloth wrapping, but that was hardly tight enough or thick enough to be waterproof. I fumbled inside my clothes and pulled it out, holding it high above the waterline.

I bit my lip as the cold water rose, to my thighs, then my waist, then my chest. . . . The chill pierced my flesh like a hundred arrows. I bit my lips harder, and small whimpers spilled out of the corners of my mouth. I had thought cold was numbing. Why wasn't I numb? My arm and shoulder began to ache with holding the *Handbook* high.

"Tilda, come back!" A voice floated across the water, pleasant, cajoling, warm. I looked over my shoulder and spotted Sir Egin. Neither he nor his horse showed any sign of planning to join us in the river. We were, for the moment, safe.

Well. Safe from Sir Egin. My flesh was finally beginning to numb—a welcome relief from the stabbing prickle-pains from the cold water—but I could no longer really tell where the fingers of my right hand were, or what they were doing. I prayed they were yet twined in Joyeuse's mane. My left hand was still above my head, clenched around the *Handbook*.

Seen between Joyeuse's ears, the far shore didn't seem any closer. Joyeuse was swimming all out, but it seemed as though we were never going to make it across, even with Sir Egin diminishingly small on the shore behind us.

If it had been any other river, we would have reached the opposite shore already. But the Rhine is vast. They say no one has bridged it this far downstream since the Romans, and even then, people doubt that the Romans built a real bridge—maybe just a series of floating rafts or something. Not a stone edifice, nothing that had lasted like so many other things had lasted from the days of the great Empire. The unconquerable Rhine was a reason that the Romans had been content to let this river be their border . . . and we were in the middle of it in December.

Currents buffeted us, tried to remove me from Joyeuse's back, but my fingers were locked on her mane. I couldn't have moved them if I'd wanted to. An occasional chunk of wood or ice struck my legs. The pain was both distant and intense—distant because of the numbness I felt, but it also hurt so much more because of the cold. I guessed other branches and such must be striking Joyeuse, but she swam on, flowing with the current but moving swiftly forward. Her steady, steaming breath was my only source of hope and sanity. I wanted to panic. We had so far to go, and I was so cold.

My arm began to tremble with the effort of holding up the *Handbook*, until I thought to rest it on my head.

I closed my eyes, hoping that by the time I opened them again, we would be across. But then I opened my eyes, and we were still in the middle of the river. So I closed them again. And again, opened them to the middle of the river. I did this over and over and over, and the world seemed a little less bright every time it reappeared.

There has to be a way, there has to be a way, a way across. The words galloped around my head over and over. There was no telling the words to go away. I couldn't think of anything outside the words, and the water, and the cold, and the current, and the rhythm of Joyeuse's swimming legs as they rocked her body beneath me.

. . . *a way, way, way across* . . .

I closed my eyes, ordering myself to think of something else. Anything else. Declensions: *Minimus. Minimī. Minimō. Minimum. Minimō. Minime.* I imagined writing the words, imagined the satisfying scratch of pen on parchment.

I forced my eyes open, surprised for a moment to realize I was on the back of a horse in the middle of a river. I couldn't believe I'd asked Joyeuse to do this. I couldn't believe how cold I was, and that I still managed to breathe.

The motion of Joyeuse's swimming faltered. I inhaled sharply and braced myself, afraid that something had happened to her—there was a jolt—then she gained her footing and lifted us out of the river.

Cold water sheeted from us as she picked her way from shallows to shore. She ran up the steep slopes of the right bank of the Rhine, into dense forest and far from the eyes of our enemy.

I lost track of everything then, I confess. I slumped forward onto Joyeuse's neck, curled around the *Handbook*, huddling close to the horse for warmth, trying to make myself as compact as possible. I didn't think that Sir Egin would be able to get to a ferryboat fast enough to pose an immediate threat to us, and I didn't think he'd bother to pursue Father Ripertus and Durendal. But I also wasn't really thinking at all. *Away*, was my impulse. *Away. Fast.*

I don't know how long I shivered in a ball on Joyeuse's back, but I'm sure the mare's heat was the only thing that kept me alive.

chapter 23

IT WAS HARD TO KEEP MY EYES OPEN. FORESTS PASSED, and vineyards; then Joyeuse climbed a rocky slope.

It was dark.

She stopped.

I fell to the ground like a sack of turnips.

Sleep.

I CAME AWAKE SLOWLY, with my back pressed against breathing warmth. I didn't want to open my eyes just yet. Even though the bed beneath me was hard, and my nose was cold, I felt safe.

I was lying on my side, my arms crossed in front of me to hold in heat. A dream had followed me out of sleep: I had been walking down to the river at Alder

Brook. But when I had turned to look for Judith to make sure she followed me, my father had been there. And instead of getting into a boat, I had stopped with my father and sat down with him in the sun on the dock.

"You got too cold," he said. "Let me help you."

And even though he was dead and I was angry with him forever, I allowed him to put his arms around me and hold me close.

I held still, held my eyes shut, trying to recapture the dream.

But the dream slipped away, crowded out by memories of running away from Sir Egin's castle, our flight through the forest, and the swim across the river.

Sleep. I had been so tired, so cold. I was warmer now, but still tired.

I heard something then—a scraping noise, of something long and heavy being dragged across loose rock.

I opened my eyes.

I was in a cavern; a waning moon, shrouded in snow-bearing clouds, was high in the sky, from what I could see beyond the cave's broad mouth. I sat up, noting that I was surrounded by silver legs. Joyeuse.

She was sleeping on her side, snoring away like she didn't have a care in the world. Much the way I never saw her eat unless I brought her a special treat, I'd never before caught her sleeping. When we'd worried about the horses' health, Parz had given us a lesson in horse sleep. Horses doze standing up for a few hours a day, snatching time here and there, but they like to have a good, restful, lying-down sleep, just like humans, yet for much shorter times.

Well, normal horses do. Our horses never ate, rarely slept . . . and thankfully, never pooped.

And they also rescued maidens from evil knights. And swam across unbridgeable rivers in winter.

No wonder Joyeuse was tired.

I wondered what had happened to Father Ripertus and Durendal. Had they evaded Sir Egin? Were they on their way to Alder Brook? It was a three-day journey from here, at least, and who knew what Ripertus would find once he got there. What if Ivo put him in the stocks? In the dungeon?

I worked for long moments to stand. My legs didn't want to lift me, and of course, only one of my feet was fully cooperative. I staggered forward, lurching into the cave wall ahead of me, but at least it was something to cling to. I had no crutch here. I wasn't sure where I'd lost it.

There came the noise of a brief scramble, and then Joyeuse was nuzzling my hair and nickering softly.

"Ow! Horse, don't eat my hair!" I said fondly, and

reached back to pet her soft cheek. I turned. "I missed you, too."

She sniffed me over from head to foot, then seemed to be satisfied by what she found. She shook herself enthusiastically, joyfully, and practically pranced out of the cave.

"Such an apt name I gave you," I said, even as a full-body shudder overtook me. I glanced down to find gooseflesh all over my arms. I was still cold. But my cheeks felt hot, like they were flushed. Aftereffects of my time in the Rhine, I decided. Naturally, Joyeuse had no such problems.

"It's going to be a long, cold night," I said, shaking out my still-damp skirts. I clutched myself and peered out of the cave. "We have to have a fire. You can make fire for me, right, Joyeuse?"

Joyeuse made a nervous noise then. She looked past me, deeper into the cave.

"What?" I asked, looking but not seeing anything.

I convinced Joyeuse to accompany me outside, and I used her for balance as I hunted around in cloud-blurred moonlight for leaves and bracken to make a bed, and for firewood. My hands shook with cold and fatigue, but I bit my lip, stubbornly refusing to stop and lie down.

Joyeuse didn't make any more noises. I kept

foraging, also looking for food as I went. The best things I found were pine needles, some wintergreen berries and leaves, and a windfall of half-wormy hazelnuts. It was not a great meal.

Back in the cave, I made a rough hearth from scattered stones, then placed the firewood at the center. I mounded some leaves and bracken around the wood, then mounded more leaves and bracken away from the fire to burrow into. I couldn't hope for Joyeuse to rejoin me on the ground. Parz had explained that horses cannot remain lying down for long periods of time; they like a good snooze, but if they stay down too long, they die. But with no blankets, and my clothes still damp, I *had* to have another source of warmth or *I* might die.

"Joy," I whispered, and she trotted over. "Joyeuse, my feet are like ice. Strike me some sparks, friend."

She pawed at the rocks of the cave, once, twice, three times. A shower of sparks landed in my hearth, and I exhaled gratefully. I stoked up the fire as best I could, but I was exhausted. I don't know how long I closed my eyes, but when I woke again, a large fire was roaring in my makeshift hearth.

"Thanks," I whispered. I scarfed down the wintergreen berries, huddled in my nearly dry cloak, clutching my knees and facing the fire. I let the heat bake my skin tight, I was so desperate for warmth, while I picked over the wormy hazelnuts. After that, I chewed wintergreen leaves and pine needles, while my stomach grumbled about the meal.

I was going to be thirsty when I woke, but that was tomorrow's problem. I was overwhelmed by fatigue, had to lie down.

I fell immediately to sleep.

I WOKE NEXT TO daylight obscured by flying snow. All was white beyond the cave entrance. A few flakes spun in on errant breezes, but for the most part, the cave mouth was positioned advantageously and did not sit in the path of the prevailing winds.

This wasn't just a snowfall. This was a whiteout. Winter had truly arrived. I tried to think what day it was. It was about a week until Christmas, wasn't it? Maybe?

I smacked dry lips together and turned to make a silly comment to Joyeuse about finding the perfect cave, even if we didn't have any water and must be out of firewood—

That's when I noticed three things: there was a stack of firewood beside my improvised hearth; the oilcloth-wrapped *Handbook* lay near the cave entrance; and Joyeuse was gone.

I tried to get to my feet, but the world faded in color and then went away altogether. I slid back to my knees.

Then the rushing, popping blaze caught my eye again. Where had the firewood come from? And who had built up the fire? Had I gone outside in my fevered state in the middle of a dark night to gather more wood? I didn't feel exactly in my right mind now, but I would have been even more fever mad to have done that.

That, perhaps, was when I started to truly worry about myself. I was ill—very ill. Thirsty, too.

So ill and thirsty that I was hallucinating. For deep in the shadows of the cave, I could make out the shape of a beast. When the fire cast its light far enough, I could even see the gleam of shining scales.

A dragon.

chapter 24

"WH-WHAT DO YOU WANT?" I CALLED IN A TREMbling voice to the shadowed dragon. Surely I was imagining it. Surely. It had to be a configuration of rocks and light, coupled with fever.

But then the bulk shifted, and a tail that had once been a shadow unwound, and a dragon slid forward, half into the light.

It opened its mouth, and I bit back a scream, yanking a burning stick from the fire to brandish before me. This dragon was not as big as the mother dragon at Wood Ash, nor as small as the first one we'd seen. This dragon was about the size of Joyeuse, wherever she had gone.

The dragon slid from the darkness, extending a

silver goblet in its claws. I raised my torch, half in protection, half to see it better. It placed the goblet on the cave floor and backed away.

I dropped the brand in the fire, straightened my spine, and took up the cup. It was filled to the brim with cool water.

The water tasted of rock and secrets.

I drank it all.

From the dragon's mouth came a hissing, popping noise, followed by a high-pitched groan and a low growl. I threw up my arms, thinking the dragon was about to attack with flame, but then—

"*Fraizola*," the dragon said.

"Are you—are you *talking* to me?" I asked, lowering my arms. "You—you spoke! You *spoke*?"

"*Fraizola*," the dragon said again.

A barber once visited Alder Brook with a pet raven he'd taught a few human words, but it was really nothing like *this*. Of course, birds sang in their own language, right? So was this just dragon language? In the stories, the few dragons who spoke all knew human speech. But maybe that was because they were always talking to saints, who had power beyond regular folks.

"Are you asking me to leave?" I asked, levering myself to my knees, ignoring the way movement made my vision and hearing fade out, then got to my feet. I felt myself falling—cast a blind hand out toward the cave wall for support—missed it—and toppled backward. Thankfully, I landed on my cloak, and not in the fire.

I lay there panting, waiting for my vision to fill back in with color and shape, and for the empty ringing to leave my ears.

When I could see again, the dragon's face was looming above my own. We stared at each other. The dragon's eyes were as deep and dark as a forest pool lined with last autumn's leaves. Around its neck, the dragon wore a tiny gold key on a golden chain, and nestled in the midst of its—her?—head spikes was a golden circlet.

"I'm sorry," I said weakly. "I'm trying to leave."

The dragon reached forward with a green paw as big as my face and put a claw on the horsetail necklace I yet wore. I swallowed against a hard lump of fear in my throat.

"You like my necklace?" I whispered. "I, uh . . . I like your circlet."

I had not seen so many dragons yet in my time as to find them unastonishing, but I did not know, from any of my research for the *Handbook*, that dragons wore gold. They hoarded treasure, maybe even slept on it . . . but did they *wear* it?

The dragon moved her touch from my necklace to

my forehead. I held my breath, waiting for pain, for death, for claws to pierce my skull. But it was just a quick touch—light, diagnostic, like when my mother used to touch my forehead to see if I had a fever.

"*Fraizola*," I breathed in the dragon's language. I had no notion what it meant, but I used it like a prayer.

"*Fraizola ix feth abiza.*" She stared at me a long moment, then backed away to busy herself with my fire, using one long, dexterous claw to stir the fire's embers.

The dragon's every movement was slow and deliberate, as though she was trying not to frighten me. She added wood to the fire and waited patiently for the log to catch. I lay still and studied her. This dragon was every shade of green, from spring leaf to winter pine. Each scale caught the light like a tiny sculpted emerald.

When the log was too long in igniting—it was dark and swollen with water; even I could see that—the dragon arched her neck and hissed a quick spout of flame over the log. With a series of snaps and pops, the wood caught fire.

"Well, thank you," I said, incapable of any other response.

The dragon ducked her head shyly.

And then, because I was truly ill and more than

a little convinced that the dragon was nothing more than a fever dream, I closed my eyes. Within moments, I was asleep once more.

I DID NOT WAKE again until Joyeuse screamed.

My first waking sight was Joyeuse's belly as she leaped over me. She landed safely, far beyond my feet.

I sat bolt upright. Joyeuse had squared off against the dragon at the far end of the cave. The dragon was still, unspeaking, as Joyeuse issued another battle cry.

"Joyeuse, no!" I cried, struggling to my feet. I wasn't immediately overwhelmed by dizziness, but I slipped anyway. I caught myself on the cave wall, scraping my arm.

Joyeuse took a step back to me but stayed in a defensive pose. The dragon didn't move. I could barely make out her colors in the darkness; only the reflected gleam of her eyes and her gold let me know where she stood.

"Joyeuse, she brought me water. She . . . she brought me firewood." I limped along the wall until I reached the horse's neck, then reached up to touch her shoulder. "No. Friend! The dragon is a friend."

Joyeuse did not look convinced, but the mare took another step backward.

But she would go no farther. She stayed in position, firm as a boulder, all four feet planted like trees.

"Fine," I croaked, suddenly weary again. "Fine. If you have to guard me, that's fine. But I think it would be best if you remembered we're her guests, and we should give her some room." I wondered why it was that I thought the dragon was female. I think it was the feminine touches to her crown.

"Hey," I said, remembering Joyeuse had been missing for some time. "Where have you *been*?"

She wheeled about and nosed a shadow near the entrance of the cave. The shadow turned out to be a small sack, which she lipped up and brought to me.

"What—where on earth—?"

I took the sack from the horse and found three loaves. I ripped into the bread and started to chew, spitting out the occasional bit of chaff that had gotten baked in.

"How did you do it? You're amazing. Thank you," I said around my mouthful of bread. She must have robbed a bakery.

After I ate, I found my shoes and went out into the blizzard—not very far—to dig a privy hole in the snow. It was too stormy to see where we were exactly, but I thought we were atop a mountain.

Joyeuse followed close, watching over me as I took care of my necessary business. While I needed her for balance, her close, watchful attention was almost disconcerting.

"I really don't need an audience," I muttered, but that didn't convince her.

My fingers itched for my quills and parchment. I had been living with a dragon for at least a day. I had so much to write down! The firewood, and the melted snow. The way she could handle delicate objects, like the goblet, or the necklace around her neck. And how her throat had puffed out when she'd dried the firewood with her internal fires. The shades of her scales, and how they differed from those of the other dragons we had faced.

And the fact that she wore a crown and a chain! What was the key for, anyway? Did the dragon simply like how it looked, or did she lock up her treasure in a money chest, the way we had at Alder Brook?

I didn't have pens and ink, but I *did* have the *Handbook*. I pulled over the package that Frau Dagmar had sneaked to me and unwrapped the oilcloth.

The book inside was not the *Handbook*.

I stared down, shocked. The book cover was dark leather, deeply tooled in designs of horses and hounds and twining thorns, full moons and pentacles.

I opened to the first page.

THE SWORN BOOK OF HEKATE

I read the words aloud, and a cold shiver went down my back. This was a grimoire. A book of sorcery.

I opened to the first page.

> "The Wild Hunt is the right arm of the Queen of the Underworld. The furious army rides at her behest, and is made of a throng of the unrighteously killed, *eidolons* given blood of the living and water from Styx. They ride through the countryside and hunt souls, to conduct them to Hades."

I looked up at Joyeuse. "This book is about you!" I scanned forward a few pages, until a bit about horses caught my eye, which came after a lengthy treatise on the "ghastly hounds" of the hunt. "Listen to this:

> "There are many hunts and many leaders, male and female. The Hunt of the Bright One is led by Brunhild. The Hunt of the Crossroads is led by Hekate, whose host flies on the wind.
>
> "In the time between hunts, the horses disperse I know not where, and make mischief among the peasantry—"

I laughed, thinking of Upper Folkstown. "Isn't that the truth!"

"—until they are called to hunt once more."

I heard the dragon moving in the depths of the cave and I stopped reading aloud.

The next part was about summoning a Hunt. I was aghast. Who would want to summon a Wild Hunt?

There was a long, detailed bit about laying out an offering to the Hunt near the nights of the dark of the moon (the body of "a maiden with a prince's blood" would do, but offerings from one's own body were also acceptable), burning certain herbs and kinds of hair on a fire, dressing as though one was ready for a hunt, and, when the Hunt showed up—if it showed up—being prepared to challenge them to a race or a duel or an ordeal.

If you lost the challenge? You forfeited your life. If you won, you were granted whatever boon you wanted, but as boons went, your request had to be ironclad in its wording. No magical creatures liked to be summoned and bound.

"Oh, my heavens," I said. "That's what Sir Egin is trying to do. He's trying to summon a Wild Hunt!"

How many maidens with a prince's blood had Egin offered?

Seven. And I would have been the eighth.

chapter 25

"BUT WHY?" I ASKED ALOUD. "WHAT CAN HE POSSIbly want with the Wild Hunt that is worth so much . . . well, trouble?" It couldn't be easy to court seven princesses, to sign seven marriage contracts—and so on and so forth. And I was sure it must be harder and harder to get the women and their families to agree to the marriages. Especially after the first two or three times Egin had turned up a widower.

Then I remembered the contented, floaty, dizzy feelings I'd had when I wasn't wearing the horsetail necklace. Egin was a sorcerer. He had the power to cloud men's—and women's—minds. It was nothing compared to the Hunt's magic, of course. . . . That must have to do with why he wanted to summon them and be granted a boon.

The book went on about the ritual of the summoning, how one should address the Wild Hunt as a group and each hunter individually, and all sorts of things that didn't seem terribly important.

Then there was this:

> **Every seven years the Hunt must capture a young dragon to become the new guardian of the Underworld. Dragons cannot live much beyond that length of time without seeing the face of the sun, and the dragons who guard the Underworld eventually sicken and die.**

This was followed by a suggestion that if you couldn't find an appropriate offering for the Hunt, or if you consistently had no luck with summoning them, then you might try to lure them with a dragon. The problem with that was the timing; who knew the first year that the "every seven" was calculated from? What followed was a table of possible dates, which went on for pages and pages.

The narrative picked up again on a section titled "Calling Forth the Dragon from the Depths"—all it took was apparently blood and a dragon claw and a few ritual words in the dragon tongue to summon up the nearest dragon.

I eyed the darkness where the dragon dwelled, wondering if this ritual would really summon the creature from the depths of its cave.

Only a fool would try to find out. And a desperate fool at that.

"Is that why you don't like dragons?" I asked Joyeuse. "You're natural enemies, as a member of the Wild Hunt? Well. They aren't *your* enemy, but you sure are theirs."

Of course, the horse couldn't answer. But from the darkness, a serpenty, slithery voice said, "Yeeeessss."

I jumped.

"Do you—did you just speak to me?" I asked stupidly. "In human speech?"

But the dragon didn't respond again.

All the stories of evil dragons—the dragons at River Bend and Horsehead Gorge, the Tarasque, and all the rest—crowded my memory. I crossed myself, remembering that all the saints did that first, and frequently subdued the dragons just through the holy gesture or prayer.

The dragon didn't suddenly burst apart into a thousand devils or just keel over after I crossed myself.

I took in a deep breath. This was not an evil dragon. She had helped me when I was ill. She had given me shelter in her home—or at least, she had not denied me shelter—during a storm. She had suffered the presence of one of her enemies.

I didn't even know why she had shown me such kindness. Perhaps she was like Judith; perhaps she saw me as Judith saw wounded birds and baby goats. Perhaps, knowing I needed aid and succor, she had taken pity on me.

"Hello . . . ," I called, wanting to talk to the dragon further. But she didn't answer me. I took a few steps deeper into the cave, but was forced to stop when Joyeuse nabbed my dress in her teeth.

I rounded on her. "I'm going to talk to the dragon," I said. "And you are going to stay here!"

Joyeuse's ears flattened.

I took the sack that Joyeuse had brought the bread in and wrapped it round and round the stickiest, sappiest pine branch I could break off a tree without losing sight of the cave entrance. I thrust the knotted fabric into the fire to make a torch.

The moment I headed for the depths of the cave with my torch, Joyeuse came jogging after me.

"No!" I said, like I was talking to a willful child.

She stared down at me sternly, and I realized: No, she wasn't a willful child. She was a grim old nun.

"I'm going," I said. "If you try to stop me, you'll probably hurt me."

I tromped off into the depths of the cave, torch held before me, one hand to the cave's wall for stability.

She followed, of course, but she didn't interfere.

As the cave floor sloped gently down, I realized the air was much warmer than outside the cave, even so far from my fire. Was the heat from the fire being drawn down? It didn't seem possible, since I couldn't really smell smoke here.

"Hello, dragon," I called in hushed tones. In spite of my low voice, the words echoed through the cave. "It's me. Tilda."

I came to a fork. The left passage was far too small for the dragon to squeeze through, but the right was the proper size. I went right. Joyeuse followed.

My torchlight revealed hidden wonders through openings like windows, some no bigger than my head: narrow caverns full of translucent white spindles, huddled colonies of sleeping bats, pools of water vast and still. The path branched. I continued to take paths that the dragon could fit through, hoping I could find my way out again. I thought about being lost down here, forced to eat bats or mushrooms and drink stagnant water to live. . . . But long before that, my torch would go out, and I would be blind.

That way lay madness. I was just about to turn back when I heard something shift in the darkness ahead.

I raised my chin and my torch and kept going. I passed through a small narrowing into a wider cave.

I gasped. Spread before me was a vast landscape of wealth. Fields of tarnished silver pfennigs were dotted with fist-sized jewels every shade of the rainbow, from ruby to amethyst. Gold marks lay scattered like daffodils emerging from patchy snow. Here and there, crowns and torcs breached the surface of silver. A gilded Roman breastplate was half buried next to a gleaming eagle poised on a long stick.

Where had it all come from? We were not far from where Siegfried killed Fafnir—could this be the Rhinegold, the fabled sunken treasure? Had this dragon pulled it from the floor of the river—or was this some other hoard completely?

Confronted with all this wealth, I had not noticed at first that the room was lit by more than my torchlight. Above the grooved walls, there was an opening to the sky about halfway up the cave wall, and weak winter sunlight flooded in.

A small mountain of gold moved, and the dragon's head emerged. Coins sheeted from her like rain, and she rose to her full height—which was small for a dragon and still plenty big enough to kill me.

Her head reared back on her long, goosey neck, and she roared.

Joyeuse bellowed a challenge, and I cringed beside the mare. This was bad. This was *so* bad.

"Sorry!" I called, retreating. "I'm so sorry. I don't

know what I was thinking. I don't want your treasure—"

The dragon hissed at that word and advanced on us.

"I don't want any part of it! I swear. I'm a princess! I mean, I could be again if I were to return home. My name is Tilda. Mathilda. Of Alder Brook. But anyway, my point is, treasure has never really been a desire of mine, certainly not treasure for treasure's sake, though I do know the value of a good curtain wall, and I assure you, I see a lot of curtain walls here. But I—all right. Look, have you seen my horse? She's a walking piece of jewelry. And she has a big treasury of her own, though that stuff is worth more for arming knights than it would be in trade."

The dragon slowed, cocking her head to the side as though listening.

"Anyway, we'll be gone soon, as soon as the blizzard subsides, though I don't know where we're going. I need to return home to Alder Brook by Christmas, and it's almost Christmas! But I also need to rescue my friends from Sir Egin—"

When I said *that* name, the dragon's head flattened and she hissed loudly.

Joyeuse trumpeted a challenge back to her.

"You know him? He's pretty . . . awful." How did

she know him? Then I remembered what I'd read in the book that Frau Dagmar had slipped to me. "'Every seven years the Hunt must capture a young dragon to become the new guardian of the Underworld.' Did Sir Egin try to capture you? Try to use you for bait for the Wild Hunt?"

"Yeeessss," the dragon hissed.

"We have something in common, then."

"Yeeessss."

We stared at each other in silence for a long moment. Joyeuse stamped an impatient foot.

"How did you—how did you learn human speech?"

The dragon continued to stare and then raised a claw to her mouth.

"Oh," I said, disappointed. "You don't really know how to talk like a human . . . just a few words. But you understand more?"

"Yeeessss."

"All right. Thank you for taking care of me when I was ill," I said. "What's your name?"

I wasn't really expecting an answer, but she said, "Curschin."

"Thank you, Curschin." My tongue only got slightly lost in the soft sounds of the name. "We'll leave you alone now. Come along, Joyeuse."

The horse did not turn her hindquarters to the

dragon, choosing to back out of the treasury cave instead. I would have smiled, for it seemed so clear that Joyeuse's distrust of Curschin was unwarranted, but on the other hand . . . it had not been that many weeks since I had considered all dragons evil. I had assumed that Sir Kunibert didn't rush out and kill all the dragons because there wasn't a reward tied to every single dragon's death. I had, in fact, thought him a selfish man for not killing more dragons.

But I saw now that Sir Kunibert had considered dragons merely animals all along, and he—and other dragon slayers, likely—wasn't going to interfere with dragons unless there were complaints against them. Even in the saints' stories and the bestiaries, there was no reference to dragon slayers who were simply on a mission to exterminate the race.

And now a dragon had spoken to me, and had cared for me when I was sick. I was used to Joyeuse's intelligence and bravery, which far exceeded those of a normal horse; she was a magical creature, through and through. But even Joyeuse could not speak human words or use human tools. Or tell me her name.

Were dragons magical, like Joyeuse, or were they of a higher order, like humans? That was a question worth learning the answer to.

We found ourselves at a dead end. We must have turned the wrong way coming back from the treasury cave. The flickering light of my torch revealed a scattering of white tree trunks and sticks spread around the floor—or at least I thought that was what they were.

I held the torch closer. Those weren't trees and sticks. They were bones. Dragon bones?

I jumped back, slightly horrified; my foot came down onto a bone, which broke beneath my shoe, and I stumbled. I caught myself against a wall and looked down to see what I'd broken. It was some sort of wing bone. I had snapped off the very end of it, which resolved into a long, thin claw.

I picked it up and held it like a pen. It was pointed at the end, though, so it really would be better as a stylus for a wax tablet than for ink and parchment. But it balanced perfectly in my fingers, curving just slightly around the bones of my hand.

It felt like magic.

By the time we backed out of the dead-end cave and found our way to the opening, the storm had finally blown over, leaving behind a calm, white world.

We went out right away. It was the first time I'd had a clear view outdoors since we'd arrived.

The cave mouth was at the top of a promontory. To my left stretched endless forest. On my right, the Rhine flowed far below us, almost straight down a steep escarpment. A small waterfall nearby had frozen in the midst of its breakneck descent to the river.

There were no boats down on the icing Rhine, and almost no signs of human habitation anywhere—except for a little building in the bend of the river on the opposite shore, complete with a small tower for setting warning lights at the shoreline.

There was only point on the Rhine where anyone felt the urge to light warning signals, and that was the narrowing at Mount Lorelei—which was famed for its murmuring waterfall. That's where I was, then—in the cave of the dragon at Mount Lorelei.

The dragon was altogether pleasanter than stories would have her seem.

Joyeuse made an uneasy sound.

"Tilda?" a voice said from behind me.

I whirled around, frightened. I saw a figure in the trees, a figure with short, golden hair. Branches obscured him, but there was no mistaking him.

"Parz? Parz!"

I ran to him, planning to throw my arms around him and hoping he'd catch me if I fell—but behind me, Joyeuse screamed a challenge.

I skidded to a stop, almost losing my footing in the snow, bending to catch myself at the last moment.

That's when Egin stepped forward from behind Parz, or maybe Parz had never been there at all, and it was just part of Egin's sorcery, because when I blinked, Parz was gone.

Egin pointed his blade at my neck until a half dozen of his men melted from the trees.

"Hello, Mathilda," Sir Egin said. "You—horse! Stay back, or she dies."

chapter 26

I HAD BEEN BACK IN MY TOWER PRISON AT THORN Edge for about an hour before the door lock clicked and Frau Dagmar stepped through alone, bearing my crutch.

I couldn't help myself. I ran to hug her. She'd tried to help me in her own prickly way. She had given me *The Sworn Book of Hekate*, too, at some personal risk.

She hugged me back, then pushed me away at the shoulders to look into my face. "I'm sorry to see you've returned," she said, but when she tried to say more, whatever magic spell choked her set to work, and she strangled on the words until she stopped speaking.

She leaned over, hands on her knees, panting as

though she'd run a long race. I stood at her side, rubbing her back. "I'm sorry, too, but I'm glad to see you hale and hearty after my escape—you weren't punished?"

She shook her head and tried to wink one streaming eye at me.

"What happened to Lord Parzifal when Father Ripertus escaped?" I asked.

She shook her head again.

On impulse, I reached behind my neck and untied the horsehair necklace. I held it out to Frau Dagmar. She looked horrified and raised her hands to ward it off.

"Don't go giving me your things, Illustrious. It's not over yet. Not nearly over."

"Just take it, for a minute." I hoped it would overcome her enchantments long enough to let her speak clearly, as it had helped me think clearly around Sir Egin.

Dubious, she took it, holding it pinched between her fingers.

"Now—where is Lord Parzifal? And my servant Judith?"

"In the dungeons," she said readily. "Don't you worry. I've given them extra blankets and good food to shore them up against the cold and damp."

Frau Dagmar took better care of the prisoners in

Thorn Edge than Sir Egin took care of his own people here.

I loved Frau Dagmar in that moment—not in a full, complete way, the way I loved Judith or my mother—or Parz; but there's a kind of love that comes from gratefulness for help that is given to your loved ones. It struck me, then: this was one of the reasons people might love their rulers. It comes from trust and belief and faith in them, that they will take care of the people you love, in ways you cannot.

She had spoken about the dungeon before she thought, but now a look of wonder came over her face, and she clutched the horsehair necklace tightly.

"I'm under a spell," she whispered. "I cannot speak of Egin or any of his doings. I cannot tell you that my words burn unspoken in my throat whenever I try to speak of him!"

Her broad, ruddy face had drained of color, and she groped for my stool and sat down. "Princess," she said, catching my hand. "You've broken the enchantment!"

I stared at her. I had known I could think more clearly when I wore it, that I had avoided Sir Egin's persuasions when I wore it; I hadn't been certain it might break the sorcery on the servants. "No," I said slowly. "It's the necklace, not me."

"You gave me the necklace, and I can speak freely

again—for the first time in years."

"You once indicated you were a prisoner here, too."

"We all are, all the servants. When we try to talk of leaving, we can't. When we try to talk of *anything* he would not want us to talk about, we can't! And when we try to leave, we grow confused, and . . . forget to leave. All we can do is dream of leaving—dream in silence." She stroked the necklace. "Did you find this cure in the book? That's what I hoped would happen, that you'd find the way—"

"No—no. The book was about something else, not his sorceries. The Wild Hunt, mostly, and a little about dragons. I'm sorry you risked so much for me and it came to so little. But thank you. Thank you for the risk. Thank you for helping Judith and Parz."

She nodded.

"Do you know—do you know when he's going to kill me?" I asked.

"At the dark of the moon, like all the others," she said.

"All of them?"

Her mouth twisted. "He's says, 'It's a lucky time to get married.' Every time. And kills them on their wedding night."

I stared at her, thinking. At the dark of the moon . . . "Take the necklace," I said on impulse.

"What?"

"Take it. Don't try to figure it out, just use it. Take that necklace and see if it breaks the whole enchantment on you. See if it lets you leave Thorn Edge."

Dagmar looked stricken. "No. No, I can't." She held it out to me. "There's no way you can escape again; he has guards posted everywhere, and they're armed to shoot you on sight. You should keep it, to help resist him."

"He'd kill me that easily?"

"The guards aren't to shoot to kill; just to wound you."

I laughed helplessly. "Well, you see? In the end, will it matter if I'm under his enchantment or not? He'll still kill me."

"It might! Maybe his plan—whatever he's killing all these women for—won't work if you aren't willing. All the others were willing."

"No," I said. "Willing or unwilling, I'll be dead all the same. You—you take the necklace. Use it to free yourself."

"I won't," she said staunchly. "I won't leave you."

I knew then the exact thing that would get her to take it. She thought like a ruler—a good ruler. "Then try it on one of the others who lives here and is trapped," I said.

She pursed her lips, her eyes narrow. "That wasn't subtle."

"I know."

She embraced me again, and left.

I went to the window and stared out. The moon was not yet dark, as *The Sworn Book of Hekate* described for summoning the Wild Hunt. But . . . why were there full moons on the book's cover?

I went to bed, and fell asleep, mulling it over.

NO ONE CAME TO bring me food or to take my night pot the next morning. I paced anxiously, toying with the dragon claw and wishing I had the *Handbook* or at least a wax tablet. I wanted to write down what I had observed of dragons during my time with Curschin.

Hours later, a disheveled and angry Sir Egin brought in a tray of food and a dress. He dropped the tray onto the table and threw the dress of gold and white wool at me, and I caught it, holding it close to my chest.

"Where's Frau Dagmar?" I asked.

"Gone," Egin said. "She and all of the servants left last night."

I stared at him. "All of them?"

"All of them. If you want a servant, you'll have to put up with a soldier from my guards."

I shook my head absently to that, wondering: How had Frau Dagmar freed all the servants with just one necklace? Had she left the castle and tossed the necklace back through the gate to the next person—or was the power of Joyeuse and Durendal's hair so strong that she unwove the necklace and each hair protected a different servant?

He took a deep breath, smoothing his hair, and turned on his charming smile.

"I hope you're ready for our wedding day," he said smoothly. "*Darling.*"

I gave him a steady look. "We both know that you aren't going to marry me," I said.

"What are you talking about, *darling*?"

"Tell me, Egin: Why have you killed seven women on the dark of the moon?"

His charming smile contorted into an evil snarl. "*You,*" he said, the word dripping with anger and contempt. "You're the one who took my book."

"*The Sworn Book of Hekate,*" I said. "I've read it now. But I'll ask you again: Why did you kill seven women at the dark of the moon? Why do you plan to kill an eighth on that night?"

"If you read the book, you know why. Immortality. The Hunt will give me immortality."

I shook my head. "I don't mean your *reason*. Seven times you failed to call the Wild Hunt. Seven times, and you never truly varied the timing of the ritual. The eighth time, and again you've made no plan to vary it."

"The fault is not the ritual, the fault is in the women. In my wives. I married among the Illustrious, daughters of princes, but they were never sovereigns. Never true rulers like you, never girls who had sat in judgment of others or given things up for people they barely knew." His lip curled, as if to say he had nothing but contempt for true rulers.

"You know nothing of what makes a true ruler, Egin."

"Oh, spare me your preaching. You're not going to redeem me, make me see the error of my ways, turn me into a noble and good—"

"I'm not trying to redeem you!" I said. "I'm *trying* to gloat."

Finally, finally, I had surprised him. "Gloat about what?" he asked. "I wouldn't think that's in your nature. *A princess doesn't gloat—she is gracious in victory.* Or some nonsense like that."

"Don't confuse my training with my nature. I wanted to tell you—it's not your wives, Egin. The fault is yours. The time to summon the Wild Hunt is any time *but* the dark of the moon."

"The book is explicit about the timing of the ritual."

"The book is wrong! I told you my own story, and I'm sure Judith told you the same one if you asked her: we met the Wild Hunt near the full moon. Not on it, but near it. You never even considered after you heard this that the book was wrong—that some scribe long ago changed something because he didn't like the material, or that the original writer may have decided use a code to hide his secrets. The front of the book is etched with full moon, for example. You've studied the book for years, but never once did you think to try to vary the timing?"

He stalked over to me and grabbed the dress that trailed loosely in my fingers, pressing it more tightly into my hands. "Get dressed," he barked.

"What—what's happening?"

"I am going to *vary the timing*," he said through clenched teeth. "Tonight."

He left, locking the door behind him.

Air no longer wanted to come into my lungs all the way. I pressed my hand to my suddenly panting chest, trying to calm my gasps, but it didn't calm my breath.

I was going to die tonight.

chapter 27

I SUCKED IN ALL THE AIR I COULD, THEN HELD MY breath by plugging my nose and putting my palm over my mouth. My lungs rebelled after a few seconds, and my breath exploded out, but I'd regained control of my breathing.

"I am not going to die tonight," I said aloud.

But I didn't believe it. I didn't eat from the tray Egin had left.

I did think to put on the dress he'd brought, though; it was considerably warmer than the dress I was wearing, and far cleaner. I washed the best I could with the little water I still had, then pulled the dress over my head.

As I thrust my hands through the sleeves,

something scratched my right arm. "Ow!" I furiously turned the sleeve over to find a pin stuck in it—holding in place my necklace. I stared at it, puzzled, even as a small line of blood welled on my skin from the scratch.

"How did you do it, Frau Dagmar?" I wondered, and put the necklace on. I couldn't guess.

But I did know, now, how I had resisted him throughout our confrontation. I had been holding tightly to the dress, and thereby holding tightly to the necklace.

I wished I had a knife—any knife—but all I had was the long claw I'd taken from the cave at Mount Lorelei. Egin might take my blood for his sacrifice, but perhaps I would take some of his first.

When the door lock clicked, I didn't get off my bed until it was insultingly obvious that I wasn't going to curtsy. Then I stood to face Sir Egin, crutch under my arm.

"Where's the priest?" I asked, making a great show of peering out the door.

His sneer was amused. "Not coming." He grabbed my arm and pushed me ahead of him down the stairs. "We're not getting married. It's unnecessary . . . there is no father coming to save you, no brothers to ride to your rescue. So strange that you are so unprotected, when you are the first one to see through my beguilements, my first unwilling girl. The previous seven came to me as docile as lambs to slaughter. But you, my eighth, are my most difficult."

"I'm not difficult," I said. "I'm just not insane."

"Oh, unfair, unfair!" he tutted as he kept pushing me down the stairs. We were well below the surface of the castle now, and I wondered if he was taking me off to some cellar or dungeon for his ritual. "They weren't insane—just beguiled. Bespelled. They wanted nothing more than to hold me in their slender arms, stroke my hair so tenderly, and call me husband. Now. Go. Through there."

He pushed me through a doorway into a dank, dark passage that smelled of rock and water. There was barely enough light to see by, and I stumbled.

"No tricks, or I'll gut you here and now!" To show he was serious, he pressed the point of his dagger into my stomach. Not far—less than the width of a fingernail—but far enough that warm blood spread across my belly.

I was frightened then. I had been frightened before, but this was when true fear took me. I let him push me forward, and stayed upright thanks only to my crutch.

A small whimper escaped me, but I clamped down on my emotions, pretending giant iron bars came around my body, squashing my heart and my lungs and my stomach in all together. I didn't have to feel anything as long as the iron was there—nothing except the squeezing.

Something cold and damp touched my face, and I almost screamed. I forced myself to breathe deeply and slowly, because if I did anything else at all, I would lose control utterly. And if I lost control of myself, I would never get free.

I took another breath, smelling marzipan and sweet wine on Egin's breath. The wetness on my face—it was a hanging vine of some sort. Egin had pushed me through a cave and outside, onto a small promontory. The cliff was encircled with trees, whose bare winter branches blotted out patches of stars.

Ahead of me, I saw a wide, dark stone altar. Underfoot, my shoe crunched on something.

On bone. I remembered from the dragon's cave what bone felt like underfoot. I let out a shrill gasp of fear.

This was it. This was my last chance. The words of the dragon summoning came to me then from *The Sworn Book of Hekate*. Could I find aid in this moment, a frail hope for survival?

I yanked the dragon claw from my sleeve and turned, slashing wildly at Egin's neck, crying out the words from the book, calling forth the dragon from the deep.

I caught him under the chin, and his blood rained down on me.

The blood burned. I screamed.

chapter 28

I SCREAM. I ROAR. I BURN.

Every inch of my flesh is on fire. Every bone and tendon is ignited from within. My brain burns, my liver burns, my heart. I roar.

There is a little creature in the place with me, and he is a lie. He glows with a lie. He has one shape around him and another shape underneath, and I can see both shapes for what they are. Both are ugly.

He is bleeding. He presses one hand to his throat, to hold in the blood. With his other hand, he holds a weapon. An edge. A sword. Thoughts are not so much words anymore, though I can't think why thoughts should be words. Thoughts are images. Thoughts are smells.

He is waving the edge. The sword. The edge? I can't remember the word! I lift my great hand and push him aside. I feel he should meet the wall. And he does. Hard. He falls to the ground in a heap. The edge bothers me, gleaming and bright, and I pick it up in my hands and snap it in half.

I am strong.

And I don't belong here, in this place of death. I can smell the bones of humans all around me, even over the stench of the man who wants to kill me and the stink of his metal.

In the distance, I hear horses and thunder, and I know I do not want to face them.

Also, there is something I meant to do. I can't think what it is, though. All I know now is that I must get away. I cast about me on all sides, looking for escape, but my body is uneasy with itself, and I cannot imagine climbing rocks straight up and down—not just yet.

So I go back the way I came, sliding into the cave as easily as a fish in water, and run the length.

The cave is not darkness to me. I can see the light in the stone here, but too soon I come to a place where the cave is not cave anymore, but human fashioning—a squareness where there should be no squares.

I break through the doorframe, leaving a small pile of stones behind me. I broke the stonework. Which is as it should be. Rock is not meant to be square. Rock is meant to be rock.

I climb stairs, up and around, up and around, and then burst through another doorframe, shattering it with happiness and satisfaction.

I am outside again. There is sky above me, but still there are walls all around, square walls. I have wings—I feel their unused weight on my back, and their untested muscles sing to me—but I don't know how to fly. I barrel straight for the great gate.

The door is barred to me. It is a door made of iron. I try to push it down, but I guess I'm not strong enough. This is a little surprising to me. But then I look at my hands and understand that they are *hands*, meant for delicate work, and that my tail is the source of my strength. I whirl about and slam my tail into the portal. It flies out. It falls down.

I leave the castle at a run. There are scores of men around the castle. I am confused. I do not remember there being scores of men around the castle before, when I had a girl's face. They shout with their weak lungs, and possibly it is supposed to be a roar, but it is no roar that makes sense to me.

These men have edges. One comes at me. I lift a hand and swat him aside, and it is satisfying to watch him hurtle through the air. I could kill him. I don't, but I could.

There are more men coming, and I hear their dogs. Enough men, enough arrows and edges, and enough dogs, and I might be in danger. But I'm not in danger yet.

I roar back, wordless roars. All these men and their edges are frightening. I am not meant for men and edges. I am not meant for walls and rules.

I am a dragon.

chapter 29

I FIND A FALLEN TREE IN THE FOREST—A ONCE-powerful oak that has been ripped up at the roots by a great wind. There is a huge shield of roots and dirt rising above the hollow carved out by the rupture. I slide into this hollow with a sigh, and I nestle against the tree roots. It is not a cave, but it will do.

I am exhausted, disoriented, confused.

I lay my heavy head down between my hands.

There is something I was supposed to do.

I close my eyes.

In the distance, I can hear the sounds of men fighting. Edge clashes on edge. I try to block out the noises. I should be running, but I cannot think of where to, until I remember the cave on the other side of the Great Flow.

It would be hard to run there, with the Great Flow between there and here.

It seems to me that it is unusual that I can run with ease.

I flex my right hind foot. It stretches all the way. I bring it up to stare at it. It looks like a foot. My ear itches, and I use this foot to scratch it.

All of this seems wrong, and seems right, too.

I do not think I sleep then, but once I put my foot down, the word-images overtake me, and I put my head down again and let them come.

THE NOISE OF THE distant strife dies away. Creatures approach. My ears pick out the noise of hooves coming. They are hooves shod with metal, but not human metals. I know these hoofbeats, though I have never heard them like this before, with such clarity and at such a distance.

I listen for the creatures. Horses. The silver horse is one of them, the horse that brings me joy. I know her by her gait. The horses and their riders are not coming right toward me. They are searching. They do not know where I am. They are going to walk by on the wrong side of the tree roots. They will never see me if I don't step forward.

My claws itch to possess the silver horse, and it

is frightening to me. I want to watch her under the sunlight.

The riders are calling a name. "Maaah-tilll-daaaa. *Tilll-daaa!*" It doesn't seem right, but I know it's my name. It's like listening to things underwater. Not in the way the noise is distorted, but in the way the words don't match up with the way I know they should sound.

Maaah-tilll-daaaa is my name.

Mathilda.

Tilll-daaa.

Tilda.

But no. These are not my names anymore.

One of the horses and her rider are close. They see me. I stand up. I am not sure if I should fight. When I had a girl's face, I loved both of these creatures, the rider and the horse, but I don't know anymore what I'm supposed to do. When I had a girl's face, the things I loved could hurt me by not loving me back. I'm much stronger than that now.

When I rise from the forest floor, the horse rears and trumpets a warning. The boy shouts: *It's the dragon!* The horse backs a step away from me, nose up and scenting the air, but the boy raises his shining edge.

My head lowers, teeth battle ready. I see the thousand ways to win if we fought. The boy would be easy to defeat. I could just open my jaws and kill him with one bite. I could stab him through with my claws. I could turn aside and whip him with my tail, and break his bones into tiny pieces. I could, if I could figure out how, blow flame to char him to ash.

The horse might claim victory over me, though. I remember, somehow, that flame does not char her. Whipping her with my tail would not work either.

But I do not fight them. I cannot fight them. I step backward, then step backward again. The horse advances on me, nostrils still flared and sniffing, eyes wide. I raise a hand full of delicate claws to stop her, even as I scrabble backward.

Where is Tilda, dragon? What did you do to her? the boy shouts, brandishing his edge.

What did I *do* to Tilda?

The boy tries to spur the horse, but she plants her feet strongly on the forest floor. *Go, go!* he cries. *Joyeuse? Advance! Why won't you fight?*

The horse drops one shoulder abruptly, and the boy tumbles off, losing his edge to the leaf litter. He rolls to a stop against a tree but leaps up to face me, unharmed, fists clenched.

By then the horse has moved toward me, whickering softly.

I wait. Her nose touches the crown of my head, and her breath is gentle warmth against my scales.

The boy stares. *Joyeuse, what are you doing?* he

asks, but he stops speaking and comes closer.

The dragon didn't eat Tilda. It is *Tilda.*

The boy I knew when I had a girl's face comes toward me. And I let him.

Oh, Tilda.

And the boy I knew when I had a girl's face reaches out and touches the thing around my neck. The necklace made from horse's hair. He's so weak, I can barely feel his touch. His hand on my throat is a rabbit's paw of softness.

How did you do it? What did you do? Come back to the castle, Tilda.

His eyes, watchful as a hawk's, leak water.

They had the castle under siege for the last day, but you broke it. We beat Sir Egin. He's gone, fled. Your steward from Alder Brook? He's here with all your knights and all your neighbors' knights. Even Sir Kunibert is here. Everything is over.

I don't have images for everything he says. It doesn't make sense, all of it.

I listen to the horse instead. The horse is snorting at me. I have to stop from reaching for her with my claws. I cannot possess her. She will fight me if I try. She is silver! Silver, which is nearly as good as gold.

I turn aside my desires. She is not *real* silver, I remember, and I remember too that once I was smaller than this horse. We are the same size now. I remember that once, I wanted to run like this horse.

I can, now.

I start to run, downhill, down the steep gorge to the Great Flow.

The boy shouts behind me, but his words don't make any sense. I think once I would have been sad to see water in his eyes. I think once, if I had known that it was I who caused it, I would have leaked water, too.

It is good to be so strong. Soon, he is gone from sight.

I do not stop when I reach the river. I remember this water from a time before, and I rear up.

The great wings on my back spread wide. I have not thought much about them since I became a dragon, but now they catch the air and lift my body.

I let out a squawk of astonishment as I rise into the air. But then my body starts to drop, and my back claws touch the winter-cold water. I paddle my feet, half running, half swimming, afraid to enter the water—but then I flex my *wings* and my body rises!

Up, down, up, down. I skim the surface of the Great Flow, water sheeting from my feet and turning to icicles, until I reach the shore and turn north, north, to the cave.

I MUST FIND THE other dragon.

I slink through the cave, inhaling the fading scents

of the old fire and sweat from when Mathilda stayed here.

Tilda.

I can picture her in my mind. She is small, but many are small compared to me. She is small beyond that, small in comparison to others like her. Her dark-golden hair is short. She hated her hair. Why could it not be red or black or gray? Some color other than gold.

This is odd. *I* love gold. It is the most beautiful color, like the sun that feeds the fire in my belly. I can *feel* gold, I think. There is some in the deep cave before me.

Tilda-girl and I agree on something else, though. She hated her foot, the twisted foot that made people think and say and do things that they would not do to any straight-foots. I hate that foot, too.

But I am stronger now. I am a straight-foot now, and I could bite the people who do not like Tilda.

Where is the other dragon? It is lonely without her.

I run through chambers vast and deep, seeing sights with my dragon eyes that I could only dream of as a human. Every rock is rich with color and shape, texture and beauty. But I cannot pause to gawk.

The only time I stop is when I find the bones of the great dragon. I stop and smell them, but there is not enough scent left to know who this dragon was. I am lonely, thinking of how he must have dwelled here alone. I am more sober but no less urgent in my searching as I go on.

But when I reach the treasure chamber, where the piles of silver and gold are glittering and alive, I forget about the other dragon.

This is *gold.* I want to lie upon the piles, to cover them with my belly, to feel the coins and nuggets shift beneath my scales. I cannot imagine a bed more comfortable.

But the other dragon is here. She shrieks at me, and comes to fight, her body in the arching S of an attack. I should retreat, but the impulse is too strong. I cannot resist! I snatch a clawful of gold from the pile and, clutching it to my chest, run away.

With a roar, she is after me, screaming, "Thief! Thief!"

She chases me through the caves, deeper, then shallower, then deeper again. Twice, her claws catch on my tail. The first time, my tail skids free. The second time, a talon rakes a dozen or more scales from my flesh. The raking feels like fire. I can hear the individual scales pinging off the cavern stones as I pass.

I drop the coins I took and I howl.

And I keep running.

⚘

SHE STOPS PURSUIT WHEN I drop the gold, probably pausing to collect it and return it to her hoard.

Out of sight of the gold, I feel ridiculous and stupid. How could I be so foolish, stealing someone's gold, just because I . . . wanted it?

I slink toward the surface, find a small cavern that fits me perfectly, and curl up inside it. The stone is comforting around me, but not as comforting as gold would be.

I am alone.

SOMETIME LATER, I HEAR the other dragon's voice hissing around corners. "Come out, thief, come out . . . ," she says.

The voice draws closer.

"Come out and face your death. Be burned to cinders for your sins. Come out. . . ."

Later: "Come out, and I will give you gold, little sister. . . ."

But I know if I come out to face her, she will not give me gold. She will kill me for trying to steal from her. That is the dragon way.

I lie still, barely breathing. Her voice retreats.

chapter 30

I DO NOT DREAM, BUT YET, PERHAPS I DO.

A human is mewing in the distance; voices bounce and scrape along the walls of the cave.

Tilda! Mathilda!

Without knowing why, I slide from my cavern and wend my way toward the call.

Tilda!

That is my name.

I should battle this human, I think, then shake my head hard, trying to clear it of these slippery, dragonish thoughts. I am not a killer. I do not battle humans. I *am* human, under all this flesh, under all this scale.

I force myself to draw closer to the call of my name, fighting my dragon fears and dragon thoughts. I come into the brightness of the cave where I once stayed.

A woman is there. I hiss, neck flat. How dare she invade this cave! How dare she try to steal the gold. That gold is *my* gold, once I take it from the other dragon.

But then I see that this is no woman. This is a girl. This is *the* girl. I grew up with her. She's the one who rescued me, with the boy.

Tilda? she says, her weak human voice quavering.

I nod, not trusting to my dragon voice or my dragon words. I step forward.

The girl speaks in the human tongue. I have a hard time understanding. But she repeats herself, over and over. *Have no fear, have no fear, have no fear.*

I settle into a crouch and wait. It is good to be near this girl. I feel better when I can smell her.

She goes for a moment and calls outside the cave. A boy comes in. I push my nose into the dirt, to keep myself from snapping my jaws at him. At them.

The girl stands beside me and has me lift my chin. The boy I knew when I had a girl's face steps forward. He is kind, I remember, and brave. He kisses me with great solemnity. His lips on mine are a bird's feather.

He pulls back and looks at me. I am having a hard time reading his expression. I know humans talk to each other through the quirks of their eyebrows and tilt of their lips as much as they do through words, but

I am having a hard time seeing these differences with my eyes.

He kisses me again.

And again.

Enough, the girl says.

I roar loudly.

The girl steps back, hands up, a defensive posture. Then she forces herself straight, faces me bravely.

Tilda! shouts the girl. *Stop that.* She steps closer to me.

I am about to strike her with my great and terrible claws when I see that she is clutching something in her tiny hands. Something brown and shaped like a doorway.

Something I want.

My strike turns soft, and I reach forward with just one claw, to touch the book in her hands.

Book. I remember this human word. I remember this book. I remember holding a pen. *My* pen.

I reach to take the book from her. She squeaks in dismay as I pluck it from her hands.

It is so small, so delicate, and I drop the book as I try to open it. I leave it on the ground, pushing at the cover with my claws, over and over. When I peel back the cover at last, I can no longer read the writing there.

When I try to turn the pages, one rips free and flutters, pierced by my claw.

The girl cries out, and so do I. I pull back my claws.

We're trying to turn you back, Tilda, the girl says. *We're trying. Kissing Parz didn't work, but . . .*

I stare at the book, at the torn page. I dig my claws into the earth of the cave floor, willing myself to stay still. I fight the urge to flee deep into the cave. I stare at the book. I stare at it and remember writing in it.

I'll never write in it again if I retreat into the cave.

Tilda, the girl says. She squares her shoulders and comes closer to me. She takes my forefinger claw into her hand. I let her, though it's hard—hard not to run away, hard not to hurt her.

Father Ripertus rallied Alder Brook and released Sir Hermannus. They came for you. All of Alder Brook came for you, Tilda. Do you understand? They came for you. *The knights sworn to Alder Brook besieged Thorn Edge. They were about to break through the gate when you broke it down from inside.*

Tilda, are you understanding any of this?

I do not really understand it, no. I do not have the best pictures for her words, and no smells, and no sense of north. It is a strange way to talk.

I find her presence soothing, though.

She takes a deep, gulping breath, hands in fists against her thighs. *If this doesn't work, we're trying Horrible next*, she says. She grasps my jaw, quick as a warrior, quicker than I can draw away, and kisses me on the mouth.

There is a long, frozen moment where I think that time has stopped. Judith's lips are touching mine, and I can hear her pulse. I can see inside of her, can see her thoughts racing. I see her fear and revulsion for the dragon shell that surrounds me. I see the love and compassion for the whole world, which she has carried around with her her entire life. The whole world, including me. Sometimes I exasperate her, but this, she thinks, is how sisters would feel toward one another, in spite of unstoppable devotion and caring.

She loves Alder Brook, loves it deeply, and cannot understand how I forgot to love it, too. It's where we were born, yes, and it's where our families are from, but that's not a reason to love it, not on its own. But it is the place that made us, made me and made her. And if I don't love myself enough to love Alder Brook, don't I love *her* enough to love *it*?

She feels as though she stands eternally at a crossroads. She cannot make any decisions until I grow up. If I never marry, she will never marry, or put it off for a long time, anyway. This is hard, because she has already chosen the names for her children—special, secret names that she does not give to kittens or baby goats.

I see all of Judith at that moment; I see all of her, love all of her, comprehend all of her. When her lips touch my scaly mouth, I see through her eyes: I view my dragon's body, with my straight, powerful limbs, my magnificent wings, my curving teeth, my sparkling eyes. But she does not see power and straightness and magnificence; she smells char on my breath and sees death in my claws. She remembers the dragon at Wood Ash slashing her leg, the fire of that pain and the fear she would die; she remembers being trapped in the cave with the young dragons; she remembers bearing the heat of flame while I crouched behind her. She is terrified, in this moment, to be pressing her lips to my muzzle.

She sees beyond this, though. And I see through Judith's inward eyes as well as her outward: I see all of myself, all that she loves and hates but mostly loves about me. I see the Tilda she believes I am, clever and resilient, surly but loving, stubborn and strong. She never pitied me for my foot the way she pities me for my dragon's body, the way she pitied me when I tore the page from my beloved book just now with my clumsy claws.

In that moment, my choices are clear, my thinking is clear. I either flee this kiss and live forever a friendless dragon, or I let the kiss return me to the feeble form I was born into. Books, pens, parchment, castles, manors, domains, accounts, pfennigs, marks, twisted flesh, painful sores, metal horses, my friends, my mother, my enemies: all weigh in the balance against freedom and gold and strength, brutality and loneliness and darkness.

Images fight with feelings. It is impossible to know which is best.

But the choice is mine.

So I makc it.

The world shatters.

chapter 31

It happened so fast, I didn't have a chance to really understand it.

The scales flew from me like beads yanked off a string, and I burned! How I burned. I roared, but my roar shrilled away to a scream. And that's all I could understand of it, before I realized that I was a girl again, and naked.

As soon as I figured that out, I crouched down and covered myself with my hands. Thank heaven for Judith: she turned me around, whisking a dress over my head and topping it with a cloak before I had a chance to think. She handed me a crutch, then knelt to help me with stockings and boots.

We did the left foot first, as usual. I pulled up the

hem of my new dress and saw my twisted foot. No healing miracles there. Just a simple transformation from maiden to dragon and back to maiden. And—and I was happy for it. Mostly. As a dragon, I'd been powerful and fast and sleek and strong, but I couldn't *think* right. I'd rather be splayfooted Tilda than Mathilda the Fiery. My mouth quirked in a grin at the strange thought, and I leaned down to pull up my stocking.

"Are you all right?" Judith asked in a low voice.

"I'm better than I was," I said, and words felt strange but so *good* in my mouth. Like proper words, not hisses and growls.

Judith nodded and helped me to my feet. I heard something in the darkness, deeper in the cave, and thought I saw the other dragon creeping back into the shadows, her eyes watchful and surprised.

Judith turned me back, and she and Parz embraced me, neither willing to wait for the other.

I hugged them in return.

Movement caught my eye, and I turned to see Horrible Hermannus ducking his head to rub at his temple. He saw my glance and bowed. "Princess," he said, making the full, deep bow that he used to give to my father.

"Sir Hermannus," I said. We stared at each other for an uncomfortably long moment.

Judith said, "Come outside, Tilda—there's a camp,

we have a fire. . . . You can have something warm to drink."

I allowed her to take me out to the fire, but not before bending down to retrieve the *Handbook* from where it lay on the ground. I plucked up the torn sheet and smoothed it out. It was the book curse, the anathema that rained down rotten noses on anyone who stole the book. I slid it back inside the book with regret.

Outside I found a busy encampment of far too many counts, knights, clerics, and servants. When they caught sight of us emerging from the cave, a ragged cheer rose up.

As cheers went, it technically wasn't very good, yet I had never heard better. And it was far superior to stone silence and a thousand signs against the evil eye.

I waved at everyone, then asked, "So who is minding Alder Brook?"

Horrible coughed slightly. "The chamberlain stayed behind."

Father Ripertus pushed through the crowd and, after a quick bow, grabbed me up into a hug. Another cheer rose from the retinue, twice as good as the first. I smiled and leaned into Father Ripertus's embrace.

"Whose kiss worked?" he asked over my head.

"You were right," Parz said. "It was Judith's."

"I don't understand," I said, pulling away.

"Come, sit *down*," Judith said, grabbing my hand to drag me to a fire.

Father Ripertus sat beside me and explained. "When Judith said she thought a kiss might be the key to the transformation, I agreed."

I glanced at Judith. "Like the swan maiden?" I asked. "But you *hate* the version where the swan is transformed back to a woman by a kiss."

Parz said, "No, that makes sense. The maiden was a swan first, a woman second. You were a girl first, and a . . . I guess Judith prefers things in their original form."

Judith glowered. "You both missed my point," she said. "I objected to the woman being *trapped*."

"Anyway," Father Ripertus said, "I thought it would be a kiss of love that would change you. . . . And I thought, what kind of love would be most effective? *Storgí*, *philía*, *érôs*, or *agápé*?"

Horrible said, "Sounds Greek to me," as he carefully maneuvered his sword to a certain position and sat down.

"It *is* Greek," Ripertus said. "The Greeks identified four kinds of love: love between family members, love between friends, intimate love, and selfless love. I thought, between Parz and Judith, you might cover the different kinds of love handily enough—oh, stop blushing, all of you. 'Intimate love' encompasses what

Plato thought about love—"

We'd been avoiding eye contact with each other since Ripertus had begun waxing on about the nature of love, but now Parz and Judith looked at me to see if I knew what Ripertus was talking about.

"Plato was a Greek philosopher," I said. "I never copied any works by him, but I have copied other things that mentioned him."

"Yes, yes," Father Ripertus said. "What I'm trying to say is, Plato thought 'intimate love' was actually spiritual—that appreciation of the beauty of another human being brought us back to the appreciation of God's beauty. Well, not *God*'s beauty. Plato was a pagan."

"I think . . . I think that was right," I said. But I didn't really think it was Judith's love for me that turned me back. I thought more it was my love for her.

A distant whinny sounded. "I think they heard your voice," Horrible said.

The metal mares burst through the trees in a thunder of hooves. They pulled up to snuffle my hair and generally make a nuisance of themselves.

Sir Horrible snorted, and I shot him an annoyed glance. He held up his hand, looking apologetic. "I'd never imagined a demon horse would come swimming up to Alder Brook with Father Ripertus on its back to rescue me; I'm still amazed, thinking about it."

"They aren't demons," Father Ripertus said before I could.

It felt like Joyeuse was combing through every lock of my hair with her teeth and tongue. I reached up to find my head wet and covered with horse slobber. I just sighed and let her continue. "So—they found you."

"They reached us about five days ago," Horrible said. "We marched on Thorn Edge the next day."

From behind me, I heard a muffled, "Move it, or I'll leave you on a silversmith's doorstep," and then Frau Dagmar appeared, elbowing aside Joyeuse to bring us a platter of cheese, fruit, and bread.

I got to my feet but stopped awkwardly short of embracing her. It was hard to hug someone carrying a platter.

She set it down and hugged me tight.

"Will you come to Alder Brook?" I asked when she released me.

"Don't you already have a handmaiden?" Dagmar asked.

"Yes, but—"

She smiled at me. "I was born to serve at Thorn Edge, and served there long before Egin was installed. I'm hoping that our liege will grant Thorn Edge to a new and better lord."

"So, Egin is—?" I glanced around the circle of faces, hoping they would explain it to me.

Horrible's expression was sober. "He's gone."

"Dead?" Had he died from the wound I'd given him? Was I a killer? I sucked in an unhappy breath.

"I don't know. He's just . . . gone. We were hoping you could tell us what happened," Horrible said.

No body had been found? Then Egin had to be alive. My bowels twisted in fear, even as I knew there was no way that Egin could reach me in the midst of all of Alder Brook's knights *and* Joyeuse. And Durendal. And Judith and Parz and Frau Dagmar.

I tried to explain the place that Egin had taken me, through the tunnels and out onto the mountainside. I tried to explain how I'd turned into a dragon, too. They all nodded and listened, but I think only the fact that they had seen me as a dragon made them believe me.

"And after you became a dragon, but before you broke through the gate at Thorn Edge . . . ," Judith prompted. "Did you see Sir Egin as you left?"

I tried to remember the order. "I snapped his sword in half. He was bleeding, clutching his throat. I heard . . . thunder. And horses."

Judith paled. "The Hunt?" she whispered.

I stared at her. "Maybe?"

We speculated on it for some time, and while we speculated, we sat down and ate until our bellies filled, while dawn broke gentle light over us. I inhaled deeply, taking in the metal scents of the horses, who still wouldn't leave my hair alone; of the smoke from the fire; of the freshness of winter's snow.

It was good to be alive. And human.

An alarming thought took me, and I sat up straight. "What day is it?"

Sir Hermannus said, "It's Saint Thomas Day."

Four days 'til Christmas!

"Everyone has been awake all night, so—" Parz was saying as I scrambled to my feet. He broke off, looking at me.

"Sit down, Tilda," Hermannus said quietly. "It's all right. There's nothing to worry about."

"Right. I was just saying we've been awake all night—there's no Thomas Donkey this year," Parz said. The last person to rise on Saint Thomas Day was the butt of jokes all day, but I was hardly worried about that.

Hermannus reached across Judith to tug my hand downward. "Tilda, all your retinue are here. I don't think there's any worry that come Christmas Eve, we're going to refresh our oaths to anyone but you. Sit back down."

I stayed standing. "Not just yet. I have unfinished business in the cave."

JUDITH AND PARZ WOULDN'T let me go alone, and truthfully, I had too strong a memory of the scrape on my dragon haunch to be easy about going to look for Curschin. The scrape had disappeared with my transformation, just as my crooked foot and belly wound had not been present in my dragon form. But now I had both crooked foot and belly wound back, though the latter had scabbed over at some point, and the former . . . well, I remembered how to deal with my foot.

Transformations were strange magic.

I did not go all the way to the treasure hoard, just stopped at a cross-passage and called her name.

She came slinking through the caverns. She blinked her dark-water eyes, adjusting to my torchlight.

"You live," she said.

"I do," I said, guarded, but also amazed that she spoke human speech so far beyond the simple, hissed *yes* from before.

She extended a claw toward me slowly. I forced myself to hold still, and the claw traced the shape of my ear.

"Human skin again," she said. "I did not know you when you first wore a dragon's face."

"You did not know me." I let out my breath. She hadn't recognized me!

"Not until I drew your blood, small gold stealer!" Her voice rose, and her posture changed. Behind me, Parz loosened his sword in its sheath, and Judith did the same. Almost unconsciously, I put my hand out, both to reassure and to stop Parz and Judith; Curschin was simply using a dragon posture to communicate possession and dominance, but not to attack.

"Tilda, what are you doing?" Judith whispered.

"She's fine! It's fine. Put your swords away. What's wrong with you?"

"What's wrong with *you*? How you're talking—this is really creepy."

"What?"

Curschin laughed. "You speak to me now in Wyrm's Tongue, small sister."

It was then that I heard it, heard the difference in words. I was speaking to her in the dragon language!

"Why did you return to this cave, small sister?" Curschin asked. "Your friends worry."

"I want to know that you do well. I want to know that you hold no grudge against me. You helped me before, and I want you to know that I am grateful."

Curschin leaned down to breathe into my face. Her breath smelled of ash and meat. "You are wise to ask of grudges. I am cave-host and water-giver to you—and you stole."

"I was—" I stopped. I didn't know the word *confused* in Wyrm's Tongue. I made spinning gestures with my hands, like winding yarn.

"Wind-snarled?" she suggested, and the word

came with a memory of wings that I'd barely used being buffeted by swirling winds. I'd never experienced it, but I could *feel* it.

"Wind-snarled," I repeated. "I was overcome by your treasure hoard. Overcome by gold-greed."

"Gold-greed is hard, for young—for new—dragons," Curschin said loftily. "You have a gold-debt to me now. I will take it from you in words. I would learn your human writing."

"Wh-what?"

"Dragons have writing, words, carved into caves." She reached out a claw and scribed some shapes on the wall, scraping away rock in a quick tumble. "When we have learned the words of the dragons who came before us, we move on to new caves. But there are few caves, and fewer new words, and I would know some other way to learn, through your books. You will teach me all the human words in the human language, and be my *wyrmgloss*, small sister." *Wyrmgloss*. A translator of dragon tongues.

I had great sympathy for her wish, for wanting to learn more, wanting to understand more. I smiled at her. "I will teach you. When I can—if I can," I said. "I'm a—" I struggled for the word *princess* in Wyrm Tongue. "I have duties. I have territories and flocks and humans to care for."

Curschin nodded, and pointed to her crown. "You

are a meat-giver. I know this strain. If you can't come to me, I will come to you. I am the one with wings."

"If you come to see me," I said, "you'll have to come at night." I hesitated to tell her I lived across the river from a dragon slayer. "You cannot scare my flocks and humans," I cautioned.

"Yes," she said. She slid into the shadows for a moment, then returned with a familiar oilcloth-wrapped book in her claws. *The Sworn Book of Hekate.* "You left this here. . . . Now tell me how to get to your cave."

"So, SHE WANTS TO learn how to read," Judith said when I told her about it on the long ride back to Alder Brook. "This is like my horse telling me her greatest ambition is to learn how to use a drop spindle. And you agreed to teach her?"

"I did."

"Explain to me again how you have a debt to her when you didn't even *get* any of her gold?"

"Dragon logic," I said. I understood it, deep in some part of me that still held a little bit of a dragon's shape. "There are laws among dragons, just as there are laws among humans. Laws govern gold and blood and debts, meat and flocks and territories, and how you deal with the rest of dragonkind." It wasn't that different from all the laws I'd spent my whole life learning. It made no less sense than chivalry; it was no less complicated than the overlapping obligations to your mother's lords, to your father's lands, to the emperor.

"But you're not a dragon anymore," Judith said, pursing her lips. "The debt doesn't mean anything to you. So why do you care if this dragon learns to read?"

I couldn't explain that I still felt the debt, honestly, not without worrying Judith that maybe my transformation wasn't as complete as it appeared. I didn't think my feeling of obligation had anything to do with that, anyway. Curschin was different from me. That didn't make her desires meaningless. People judged me based on my appearance all the time. There was no chance I was going to judge her based on hers, just because she looked like a monster in the eyes of some.

Parz rode up to us, a dazed expression on his face. "Sir Kunibert asked me to rejoin him as his squire," he said.

Judith and I glanced at each other. "What did you say?" Judith asked.

"I said, 'Not as long as some dragons are really princesses in disguise.'"

"Is he going to reconsider being a dragon slayer?"

"Noooo," Parz said. "But he promised that he would leave Curschin alone."

"But what are you going to do if you don't stay with Sir Kunibert?" I asked. "We would really miss you if you weren't across the river."

"What if I were on *your* side of the river?"

Judith said, "You asked him? He said yes?"

I frowned. "Are you two keeping secrets from me again? Don't make me cross."

Parz grinned. "I'm going to be Sir Hermannus's squire." When I groaned, he said, "And you are absolutely not allowed to call him Horrible anymore!"

I put my hand over my mouth. "Wait. I don't call him that out loud, do I?"

"At least once," Parz said.

"Lots more than that," Judith said.

chapter 32

WE CAMPED THAT NIGHT ON THE WAY BACK TO Alder Brook, being too many to stay together at a guesthouse.

I had a hard time sleeping. Wyrm's Tongue flowed through my mind as though I'd never transformed back to human, and I lay very still, frightened that I might not be able to hold on to human form.

Then I heard my name, whispered so close and so intimately that I would have thought there was someone standing right beside me and breathing hot words into my ear.

I sat up, staring wildly around in the dim light of campfires that shone through the tent walls. Judith was on her side, wrapped in all the blankets and yet sprawling. Frau Dagmar had returned to Thorn Edge, and there were no other women in the tent with us.

"Tilda," said the voice in my ear again, a dark, purring whisper.

I leaped out of bed. I grabbed for Joyeuse's silver dagger—all the horses' tack and armor had been recovered from Thorn Edge after I broke the siege.

"Come to the forest," the voice thrummed.

"Who is it?" I whispered fiercely to the air. "What is this magic?"

Judith woke. "What's going on? Who are you talking to, Tilda?"

"Come now, or the Wild Hunt will come to you," the voice continued.

And then a second voice, a voice I recognized too well, rasped, "You owe a debt to me, Mathilda of Alder Brook."

The Hunter.

A spear of ice seemed to sink into my stomach, and fear clenched my bowels.

Judith said, "What—?" but I put my finger to my lips and tilted my head to the tent flap. I didn't want to speak, in case the voice could hear me, or hear the things I could hear.

Judith pulled the copper sword from the bed—she'd been sleeping with it—and she girded herself with the sword belt. We donned cloaks over our shifts, slid on our shoes, and went out into the snowy night. I was grateful for her silent trust.

We did not *try* to sneak away from camp and into the forest; it was just that no one was watching us.

The moon was a bruise-yellow thumbnail paring just above the horizon. It seemed the stars cast a brighter light. At least the snow reflected what light there was, and we were able to walk in the darkness without stumbling. Much.

We stole deeper into the forest. A quiet hoofstep tipped me off, and when we came around the corner to find Joyeuse and Durendal, Judith and I both heaved a sigh of relief.

But our sighs came too soon. The silent night was split by a thunderclap and a light as bright as two suns. Judith and I both shouted and clutched our ears, clenching our eyes shut, until the thunder died away and witch light overtook the world.

The baying of the hounds and the call of the horn followed quickly after.

Judith and I stood silent beside the horses, blades ready, waiting. I wished I had grabbed the silver sword and not the dagger. I wished that, like Judith, I had thought to sleep with a sword.

The Wild Hunt arrived.

The great bright-dark stallion and his helmeted, red-mawed rider led the way. I was not by any means relieved by the familiarity of this moment that I recognized from my nightmares.

I craned my head, looking for the golden horse with the iron bridle. The one I had failed to free.

The golden stallion had a rider. In golden armor identical to my silver armor.

Egin.

"Tilda," he said with a smile. "I appreciate you answering my summons."

"Please tell me you have some reason for this summons other than petty revenge," Judith said.

"Hardly petty," Egin said, drawing the golden dagger at his waist.

I couldn't even figure out what my emotions were well enough to mask them. I asked the first question that dashed into my head. "Did you get it?" I asked. "Did you get immortality?"

The red-mawed rider drew closer and answered for him. "Yes. This one has been granted immortality."

Egin's grin was triumphant and ugly as he swung one leg over the golden stallion's back.

"For as long as he rides," the red-mawed rider said in her rough, whispering voice.

Egin's grin faded, even as his feet headed for the ground. It seemed he had one second of perfect realization of the terms of his immortality before his body fell into dust.

Judith screamed.

"Why?" I asked the Hunter.

"No gift which is forced to be given ever truly belongs to the receiver," the Hunter said. Her great horse snorted and stomped. "I know you have read the same sworn book as Egin, Mathilda of Alder Brook. Do not try to summon the Hunt, or you will receive a similar gift."

"Do *not* worry about that," I said.

She turned her burning face to our horses. "Cuprum and Argentum," she said. "They stayed with you."

I bit my lip, waiting for my judgment. Or punishment. Or whatever was coming.

"Finish it, mortal child. Free all three, and the debt between us will be repaid."

"It will? I thought the debt was owed for freeing Joyeuse and Durendal—I mean, Argentum and Cuprum."

"I speak now of the debt I owe to you. Egin would not have climbed down from Aurum for anything less than your murder. I am pleased he is gone. The debt I owe you now is as great as the loss of the Elysian horses."

I stared at her blankly, frozen, trying to understand her words. Judith understood more quickly than I, I confess; she walked over to the golden stallion, reached up, and pulled off the iron bridle.

"Yes," the Hunter said. "Judith, daughter of Aleidis, is your servant. That will discharge the debt just as well."

She gestured, and her huntsman sounded his bone-chilling horn. The Hunt departed, leaving the golden stallion behind.

In the sudden silence that fell, Judith whispered, "Did she call them Elysian horses? What's that mean?"

"The place in the Underworld where the heroes go to live—the Elysian Fields. I'm not surprised to find they have such wonderful horses there." I stared at them.

The golden stallion lowered his nose to Judith's hair and whuffled. I couldn't help but grin, albeit sadly.

"Now that they're all free, maybe they'll go back to the Underworld," I said wistfully.

"Ugh," said Judith. "Stop being so depressing. Look, these horses are immortal, probably. What's a few years spent with some human beings before they go back to wherever they're from? *I* don't think they're going to leave us."

As if to agree with her, Joyeuse whickered. The other horses followed suit.

"Will you stay?" I whispered to Joyeuse. She poked her head over my shoulder and chewed thoughtfully on the edge of my chemise.

I took that to be a yes.

In the morning, we pretended we did not know where the third metal horse had come from, to avoid lectures about maybe not running off in the middle of the night to confront ancient and mystical forces.

Instead, we just expressed astonishment along with everyone else.

"What's his name going to be?" Parz asked me and Judith.

I glanced at Judith, and she nodded.

"We think you should choose," I said.

Parz's eyes lit as bright as the moonstones that dotted the golden saddle. "I have the perfect name," he said. "You're going to love it. Curtana."

We must have looked puzzled, because Parz repeated himself. "*Curtana*," he said significantly. "You know how Joyeuse and Durendal were forged from the same steel—well there was a third companion sword, Curtana, which belonged to Ogier the Dane—" He stopped when he realized we were staring at him blankly.

"What?" I said politely.

"Ogier fought Charlemagne for seven years, until the Saracens came, and then he fought by Charlemagne's side." When this failed to excite us or jog our memories, he added, "Ogier killed a *giant* with Curtana."

"All right then," I said, and patted the golden horse's neck. "How do you feel about the name Curtana, my dear?"

The horse did not seem to object.

chapter 33

When we finally rode into Alder Brook on Christmas Day, it seemed both smaller and grander than I remembered. When people cheered our arrival, I felt both smaller and grander than I remembered, too.

Parz rode Curtana closer to Joyeuse during our arrival. "Look *happy*," he said in a low voice.

"What?"

"You're doing that thing you do, when you feel too much and your face just freezes into place. We who know you well enough understand that, but it's hard for people who don't."

"I don't know how to *look* happy," I said, frustrated. "They'll see through it if I force myself to smile. I'm so ashamed, Parz, that they cheer me for returning after I tried to run away."

Judith was giving us a concerned look, but Parz waved her off. "Tilda, I understand that you have not always felt as welcome and loved here as you would want, but I wonder if you have ignored some of the love that is truly here. It would be easier for people to love you if they could see that you loved them, too."

I looked at him with surprise.

He blushed, ducking his head and fingering his old scar. "What? I may not be a prince, but my family has ruled Hare Hedge since Charlemagne. I understand *some* things."

Ivo had disappeared by the time we returned; he'd seen the handwriting on the wall. But Sir Hermannus sent the marshal after him and had him dragged back for justice.

It was hard for me to agree to punish Ivo; I was too aware of my own guilt for such punishment to sit well. Plus, compared to Sir Egin, Ivo was just a usurper with no sense, not an evil murderer. Really, Ivo seemed fairly benign. But Horrible was being Horrible again, and insisted that sitting judgment on Ivo was a task for my mother, not me.

"Who is the ruler here?" I asked.

He blinked at me blandly. "Until you come of age, it's your mother, but—Princess. I understand your feelings. But learn from this. Egin's crimes are like the sun, and Ivo's are the moon. Do not think, because the sun is so bright, that the moon does not also cast light enough to make shadows."

I sighed. It was hard to hate Horrible when he wasn't wrong.

JUDITH AND I WERE preparing for bed when I burst out, "How can you stand it?"

Judith froze in the midst of rubbing oil into her hands and looked around. "Stand what?"

"Being here, with me, now, knowing what you know about me, when they're all cheering my return. . . ."

Judith went back to rubbing her hands. "Oh, Tilda," she said, as though tired of the whole conversation.

"Fine, fine; you want to keep the secret that I ran away? I can't deny that it's easier for me."

"Easier for all of us," Judith said.

"In the short run or the long run, though?"

She took a deep breath, throwing back the covers to our bed. "It's like the story of the prodigal son from the Gospels."

I flinched, stung that Judith would compare me to the younger son of the story, who wastes his inheritance on wild living.

"You're saying I don't deserve this forgiveness—this mercy?"

"Oh, that's not what I mean!" Judith said. "For one thing, mercy isn't earned. Otherwise it wouldn't be mercy. I don't think you're the prodigal son, Tilda. But—maybe Alder Brook is like the father in the story. It's just . . . glad you're back. There's no need to make things harder for you."

I bit my lip, thinking how much I owed Judith.

"Thank you," I said, watching as she removed warming bricks from our bed with long-handled tongs.

"For what?"

"For rescuing me."

Her mouth quirked. She looked up, her blue-green eyes bright and laughing. "Which time?"

WHEN MY MOTHER RETURNED home several days later, our reunion was tender at first. I was terribly relieved to have her back, healthy and whole.

On her second day back, she brought Judith in to join my daily lessons on the fine points of running a castle. "That girl is going to marry a lord someday," my mother told me. "Or run an abbey. Service is not for her, either way."

Judith hated it. "It's boring, being a lady without a manor," she said. "It makes me want to run off and become a dragon slayer again." It made the skin over my spine itch, thinking about dragon slayers.

My unease must have shown on my face, because Judith apologized. "Sorry. I mean, dragon *protector*, of course."

In the days since my return to Alder Brook but before my mother came back, I had fallen into the habit of getting up early and working on my book before appearing in the great hall. And I had instructed Sir Hermannus and Judith to allow no one to disturb me during that brief time.

But my mother found this to be too high-handed of me, and reminded me that copying work was something that should not take any precedence over my other duties.

I still felt too guilty about abandoning Alder Brook to speak up, to explain that it was no longer mere *copying* work that I was doing. As the days passed, I found myself using my mask of ice with my mother more and more.

One morning about two weeks after my mother's return, Sir Hermannus and Father Ripertus took me aside after breakfast.

"Do you want us to come with you?" Father Ripertus asked kindly.

"Come with me where?"

"For when you explain to Princess Isobel about your dragon handbook," Sir Hermannus said.

"What's to explain?" I asked. "I used to think if

I escaped to a cloister, I'd have more time to spend on books, but that's untrue. I used also to imagine I would like to be imprisoned, but . . ." My laugh was brittle. "Well, it's actually no fun at all. But I accept this. I'm a princess. This is how it's going to be."

"Your Boethius led a political life and still found the time to write his books," Father Ripertus said. "He was a senator of Rome. I think that's about as difficult as being the Princess of Alder Brook. Perhaps a little more so on some days—perhaps a little less on others. It is all about the balance."

"In no way were you shirking your duties before your mother's return," Sir Hermannus said. "I know you wrote in your history less than you wanted to, but it was still more than now. Father Ripertus is right: it's about the balance. Let's talk to Princess Isobel."

"She'll say no."

Sir Hermannus raised his eyebrows. "I wasn't suggesting you ask her permission, Most Illustrious. I was suggesting you tell her what you need."

"Need, or want?" I asked.

Father Ripertus smiled. "Need."

I hunched my shoulders, trying to imagine that conversation. "Maybe tomorrow."

I WAS RESTLESS THAT night, and rather than kick my bedmates awake with my thrashing, I wandered the castle. I wove haltingly among the sleeping figures in the great hall, taking care not to tread on an outstretched hand or an errant foot.

It made me remember the night I had restlessly wandered Boar House, before Ivo kidnapped me. I had so envied all the people sleeping in the hall that night. I almost laughed, thinking of the younger self I'd been not so long ago, when I had thought freedom meant choosing where you slept.

Of course, I hadn't been wrong. Freedom *was* choosing where you slept. But it was also choosing who you dined with, who you called friend, and what you did with your day.

It occurred to me that I was being cowardly. I was only thirteen, and had years yet before reaching my majority. I was reliant on my mother for her lessons and guidance in becoming the ruling Princess of Alder Brook. But Sir Hermannus and Father Ripertus were right. It was about the balance.

It was kind of them to offer to come with me.

I went out into the courtyard and walked awhile in the bracing night air. A cloud dimmed the moon briefly, and I was struck by a thought.

It wasn't *kind* of them to offer to come with me. They were offering to come because they considered themselves *my* counselors. They were willing to stand against my mother with me.

I paced the courtyard, considering this. My mind strayed to Judith, and her boredom with learning to be a lady with no manor. There was no reason she could not eventually take on a few of my duties; there was no reason that when I came of age, I could not carve out some small section of Alder Brook and give her a proper benefice to rule, plus a title to go with the duties and the land. Princes did this with knights all the time—turned them into counts and gave them jobs like organizing the household. Why couldn't Judith be my steward as capably as Sir Hermannus, once he retired?

The whir of enormous wings warned me, and I held very still against a wall while Curschin landed in the courtyard.

"Greetings, small sister," the dragon said. "I have come many nights, but this is the first I have seen you. I have come for my lesson."

"Greetings, Curschin." She came! She'd been coming, and I'd been too distracted to go look for her. Ever since I'd given up writing the *Handbook for Dragon Slayers* and started over with the *Historia Draconum*, I'd kicked myself for all the questions I'd never asked her when I'd had the chance.

And now she was here, and she wanted to learn from me. Almost as much as I wanted to learn from her.

Questions crowded my mouth, but first things

first. I had to honor my promise to her.

"Let us begin our lessons right now. We'll start with your name," I said. "*C* for Curschin."

She bowed her head. "Very well, *wyrmgloss*."

Lit only by the moon and the stars, I drew a *C* in the dirt of the courtyard with my crutch.

"*C* is for Curschin," the dragon repeated, and traced a *C* with her claw.

"Very good," I said, and smiled, hugging myself a little.

Tomorrow I would go to my mother with my retinue. With Sir Hermannus, Father Ripertus, and Judith at my side, I would lay out the future for her. I was going to be the Princess of Alder Brook, yes, but I was also going to write a great book.

Epilogue

The dragon is the biggest of all serpents, and of all living animals on Earth. The Greeks call it δρακον, the Latins *draco*, and in our local dialect, we call it *Drache* or *Wurm*.

There are many stories about dragons that live in caves, where they guard vast treasuries from lost kingdoms with fire and poison. Perhaps it is because of its association with serpents, fire, and poison that a dragon is thought of as nothing but a devil, a servant of the king of all evil.

But there is no instance I have seen when a dragon operates from pure evil; yet I have seen men and women who deceive with every breath, who use beauty to delude people into false hope and joy, and then rob them of that joy and hope before abandoning them to despair and death.

The truth is that, mostly, dragons are animals—smart

animals, capable of speech, with their own territories and desires. Like bears, they are protective of their young. They are predators to be respected; they are not horses nor cows, meant to bend to our service. Like humans, they can read and write and tell stories.

Of course, sometimes dragons are not dragons at all—but human girls (or boys), trapped within scales and claws. If you can overcome your fear and show these trapped creatures kindness and love, you may just discover the truth inside them.

—from Mathilda of Alder Brook's
Historia Draconum

Acknowledgments

I must thank my editor, Anne Hoppe, and my agent, Caitlin Blasdell, for their diligent eyes on this one, and for spurring me through a really bad case of second-book-itis. Thank you. I really needed you on this one.

The HarperCollins Team of Awesome, in particular Joel Tippie for the great cover design, Laurel Symonds for kindness and efficiency and all the stuff I don't even know she does, and Renée Cafiero for her eagle eye. You do amazing work, folks!

Jason Chan, thanks for that last cover; Kevin Keele, thanks for the current cover; Kathryn Hinds, thanks for the constant bacon saving.

Megan Eaton, thank you for being my official German consultant. Errors and bad choices in this arena are mine, never hers! Same errors disclaimer applies to the horse stuff, for which I must thank Lisa Cameron-Norfleet and Quincy, plus Kayla Fuller.

Thank you to my reader-critiquers: Julie Winningham, always first; Jason Larke, always convinced not enough people die in any draft; Julie DeJong, who cried for Felix and cheered for everything else; Catherine Shaffer, for being resolutely reassuring even when I had to irrationally rebuff any reassurance; Elizabeth Shack, for liking what I write; Kate Riley, for the chaos and the encouragement.

Last but never least: thanks to my family.

More from

MERRIE HASKELL

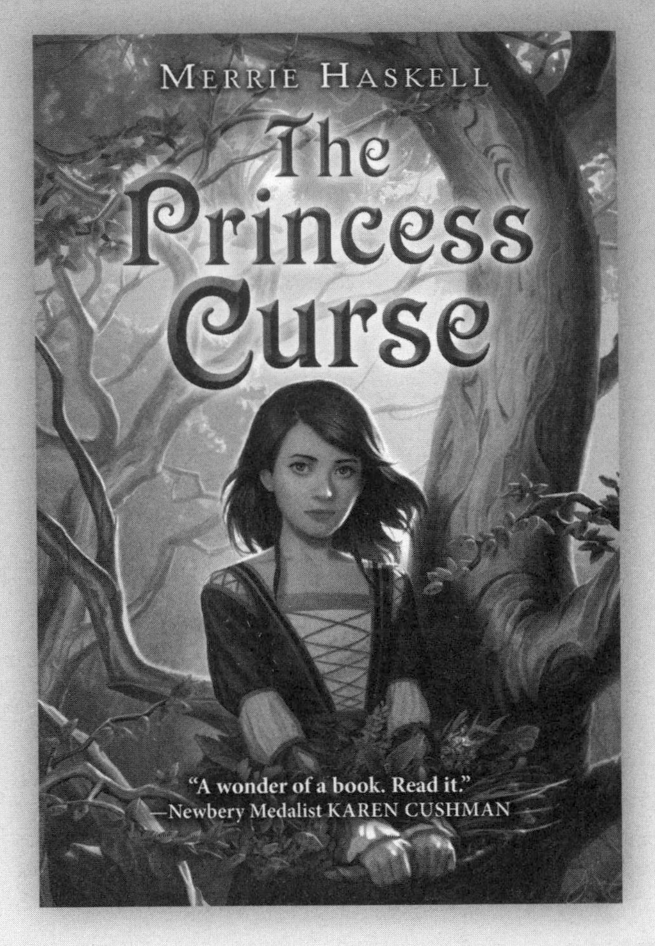

Reveka has little use for princesses, with their snooty attitudes and impractical clothing. She does, however, have use for the money being offered as a reward for breaking a curse that currently plagues *twelve* princesses. As Reveka struggles to understand the curse, she meets shadowy strangers and uncovers even bigger mysteries. . . .

HARPER

An Imprint of HarperCollins*Publishers*

www.harpercollinschildrens.com